THE MISSING INGREDIENT

REALITY OF LOVE SERIES #1

MARIKA RAY

The Missing Ingredient

Copyright © 2019 by Marika Ray

This book is a work of fiction. Names, characters, places, and incidents are products of the author's imagination or are used fictitiously. Any resemblance to actual events, locales, or persons, living or dead, is entirely coincidental.

First Edition: March 21, 2019

All rights reserved, including the right to reproduce this book or portions thereof in any form whatsoever.

Special thanks to:

Cover Design by Laura Halloran
Editing by Lawrence Editing
Proofreading by Judy Zweifel

DEDICATION

To my high school Spanish teacher with her dark hair, red lips, and extraordinary sass in a small package...

THE MISSING INGREDIENT

Who knew a cooking show could get so messy?

Elle Fierro

All I have to do is appear as a judge on this cooking show in Hollywood and my restaurant will open to rave reviews. Pretty much my lifelong dream. What I absolutely shouldn't do is sleep with one of the contestants and ruin everything I've worked so hard for. But he gives good hugs, makes me laugh, fills out a simple T-shirt like nobody's business, and is sweeter than the maple syrup he dripped all over my naked body last night...

Austin Cox

I may have been drunk when I applied to be on that reality cooking show, which is why it's hard to believe I'm here. What's even harder to believe is that Elle, with her painted red lips and fiery disposition, is in my bed and making me forget I need to win this damn show to get my little sister out of the foster care system.

When Elle throws me under the bus to realize her dream, will our love burn out or will we find the missing ingredient to happiness?

1

———————

lle

"*Dios mío...*" I muttered for the six hundred twenty-ninth time that night.

The kitchen assistant looked over at me from the side of her eyes, the slightest flutter to the knife she was currently chopping with. The sick, twisted part of me that reared its head often in the kitchen enjoyed seeing that little tremble. I was the executive chef of this three-star restaurant with reservations booked six months in advance. If I was upset, everyone should be upset. Shit runs downhill, as the Americans say.

"Take that back and make it right," I barked at the expediter about to exit my kitchen with a totally unacceptable splattering of sauce on the side of the chicken, like it had been murdered right there on the damn plate. I spun around and addressed my next comment to the entire kitchen, my Spanish accent more pronounced as the evening wore on. "If you can't plate a simple chicken parmesan without it looking like a murder scene, get the fuck out of my kitchen right now!"

Silence, permeated only by the sound of water boiling and steak sizzling, filled the air. When no one left the kitchen, I assumed they were all properly chastised and spun back around to deal with my current disaster, the swordfish supply that was running out way too early in the night. We only had two main fish entrees on the menu and for whatever reason, everyone wanted swordfish tonight. I made a mental note to talk to the kitchen manager about increasing our order for tomorrow's delivery.

The assistant manager walked by the line and I rushed over to snag her attention. "Tell your servers to push the bass. Or we'll have to eighty-six the swordfish."

Her eyes widened for a split second upon hearing we might run out. No top-end restaurant wanted to exhaust their supply of a menu item at only eight o'clock in the evening. We had hours to go and mouths to feed. To run out of the swordfish would be an embarrassment. And considering tonight was my last night at this restaurant, I couldn't allow that to happen.

I'd been with Lilalia for five years, turning it into one of New York's top-rated restaurants as the executive chef. I ran my Soho kitchen with an iron fist. I expected perfection, both from myself and from the staff I hired personally. Considering I was only five foot three and female, I had to put a bit more bite in my bark in order for everyone to take me seriously.

"El Jefe!"

I turned to find a server poking her head into the kitchen, a timid smile on her face. Everyone in the restaurant called me "El Jefe," which meant "The Boss" in Spanish. I pinkie swear I didn't order them to call me that. My first name was Elle and my last name Fierro, so if you put Elle and "F" together in Spanish, it was pronounced Elle Efe, which was very close to El Jefe.

The important thing to note here was I secretly *loved* that they call me The Boss in Spanish. It gave me a little thrill every time I heard it, like I was actually six feet tall, commanding my people from up high.

I may have issues with my short stature. I couldn't say for sure.

"What is it?" I asked her quickly. I had things to do and swordfish to pull out of thin air.

She talked rapidly, trying to spit everything out before I inevitably snapped at her. "There's a gentleman who insists on meeting the chef. Can I send him over?"

I narrowed my eyes at her and she shrank back, but still stuttered out, "I-I promise he looks reputable. Fancy suit and shoes. Just paid with a black Amex."

"Mmm." My noncommittal noise made her eyes widen, but she didn't slink away. The staff knew not to interrupt me for just anyone. If she was this insistent I speak privately with a diner, he must be someone important.

Reaching up, I pulled off my hat. "Send him over in three minutes."

I spun around, not waiting for her response, and went into the back where we all stuffed our private belongings before donning our aprons and turning into the finest kitchen staff in New York.

My LOEWE bag sat by itself in the premier locker position, as it should. That handbag cost me more than my rent. Twisting the tube of my signature deep red lipstick I always carried with me, I smoothed on another coat, making sure my full lips were perfect. A few wisps of dark brown hair were swept back into my chignon and I was ready.

One never meets a rich male without looking her best.

Mother dearest taught me all manner of things growing up, but that tenet had to be number one.

I swept back into the kitchen, smoothing down my tight apron, and flung open the swinging door before stepping through like I was on the catwalk. Always make an entrance. Yes, that's right, darling. Another life rule from Mother.

To my delight, a tall handsome man stood waiting for me. To describe him as delicious would be an understatement. He filled out his suit like a soccer player, all buff muscle and smooth moves. Perfectly gelled black hair and dark eyes completed his look and piqued my interest.

"Ms. Fierro?"

Wasting no time extending my hand, I nodded regally. "I trust you enjoyed your meal this evening, *Diablo Hermoso*?"

His huge hand enveloped mine and tugged me closer. "*Sarò il tuo diavolo.*"

The gorgeous package, the accent, and now the flirtatious invitation to be my own personal devil in Italian was all quite nice. My exact list of attributes in an ideal man brought to life and offering himself on a silver platter. Under normal circumstances, I'd be thrilled to make his acquaintance, if you know what I mean. But there was something about him that was too perfect. I just didn't feel that flutter of excitement in my belly like I should.

My step back was subtle yet he noticed. He released my hand and pulled out a crisp white business card from the inside pocket of his suit jacket.

"I would love to discuss your swordfish preparation further." His English was spot-on, despite his request being quite odd. I'm sure he had no interest in my swordfish, but rather a particular interest in getting into my bed.

I pulled the card from his fingers, not missing the way he held on much longer than necessary. "I will call you next time I feel like...discussing swordfish."

A smile quirked his thin lips before he leaned forward and kissed me on both cheeks. His stubble grazed my skin and normally that kind of intimacy would send a shiver down my spine. This gentleman? Nada.

A shame really. What a waste. A beautiful man. Pure opportunity. And yet no tingles down where it mattered.

He sauntered off, disillusioned that I'd be calling him tonight. *Lo siento.* Italy would get no love from Spain tonight.

I flung the door to the kitchen back open, my mind on why my tingly bits had seemingly left the building. I must have startled my sous chef, who clearly didn't have a mother to teach him about grand entrances, because he dropped a spoon right on the counter, sauce flying off and splattering onto my cheek.

Everyone froze, like the splatter was the shot heard 'round the world. I blinked once, the pale face of my sous chef not changing. My spine elongated and I pulled myself up to my full height.

"I'm so very sorry, El Jefe," he finally whispered. His hand extended into the space between us, a clean rag his peace offering. I accepted it, gave him a stiff nod, and then marched back out to the locker area to clean my face in private. As I passed my staff, they all averted their eyes out of respect. They knew how fastidious I was about my appearance.

We somehow made it through the rest of the night like the well-oiled machine I knew we were. Everyone was on their best behavior and we came very close, but didn't actually run out of the swordfish thanks to the servers pushing diners toward the sea bass like they'd been advised.

As usual, my feet were killing me and I was starting to come down from the high I got every time I put on an apron and ran a busy kitchen.

"You got it from here?" I asked my sous chef. He nodded firmly and despite the sauce incident earlier that evening, I trusted him. I went to the back and stowed my folded hat and apron in my handbag. A quick trickle of sadness overtook me as I packed up for the night.

Five years was a long time to give your heart and soul to a restaurant. I would miss Lilalia and everyone who worked there. Yes, I was the head chef, but I couldn't have achieved those three stars without their assistance. And as often as I tried to keep things just business, they insisted on talking about their families and personal lives, dragging me into the friendship zone, kicking my stiletto heels and screaming in Spanish. I slammed my locker shut for the last time and began my walk through the kitchen to get to the parking lot.

This time, my grand entrance was not by my design, but because of my staff. They all stopped what they were doing and spun around, hands on hearts as I walked through them. The backs of my eyes began to sting and I could feel my chin wobble. When I got to the door, I spun around and took them all in, still at attention with eyes on me.

Breaking my code of all-business-all-the-time, I smiled at them with all the love in my heart that I never allowed to show. I bowed, the sweep of my head my thanks to them for years of impeccable service. Then I lifted my hand and blew them a kiss.

I walked out to applause.

The tears came as I walked across the dark parking lot to my car. I swiped them away before anyone could happen to see. Showing emotions was definitely not one of the tenets taught by my mother. I really had nothing to cry over anyway.

My future was bright. I was leaving Lilalia to go to Hollywood and record a reality cooking show called Taste Test. I'd been invited to be one of the three head celebrity judges, an honor that would get me the type of press I'd need in order to come back to New York and open my own restaurant. The space was already purchased and my contractor was building it out. I just needed to get enough buzz going to make sure the line was out the door. With this reality show, I'd be set.

Everything I'd dreamed of since I took my first cooking class in a little restaurant in Spain at ten years old was coming true. All the derision over the years from my mother for picking a profession that required getting sweaty and actually working was finally paying off.

"I'm not a short order cook, Mother, I'm a fucking celebrity chef with my own restaurant," I muttered to myself as I drove away from home for the last five years.

My eyes were leaking because I was proud of myself. Because my staff cared about me. I'd made a difference, I'd left my mark, and that felt good. I'd miss everyone I yelled at every night, but I had plans that made leaving inevitable.

After parking in the private lot I paid extra for, I let myself into my tiny apartment. It wasn't that I didn't have the money for a much bigger place. I did, thanks to Mother dearest and her many years of modeling. It's just that I didn't like being alone in a huge place, pin-balling around with no people to absorb the noises and make the space a home.

After changing into comfortable silk pajamas, I pulled out two suitcases and started layering my clothing into them. The producers told me to plan for a couple weeks, though they'd condense the taping into as few days as possible. How a woman could possibly pack for several weeks was beyond me, but I did my best.

I packed shoes, each in their own bag to prevent scuffs that invariably happened when you traveled via airplane. I'd traveled quite a bit internationally with Mother, so I knew what kind of damage could be done. I chose three handbags and wondered if that would be enough.

Dumping out my LOEWE bag from earlier, I saw the business card from the Italian. I picked it up and fingered the sharp edge. I considered calling him for a nice distraction after all. Sort of a "farewell for now" gift for myself.

But then the sensible side of me worried about getting enough sleep before my long flight. Which then led me to wondering when the hell I'd gotten so old as to turn down a gorgeous male in trade for beauty sleep.

"This is it then, huh? You've gotten old, Elle," I said to myself in the full-length mirror in my bedroom. Yes, I was wearing silk pajamas, but they were pants, not a pretty nightie like I used to wear prancing around all manner of hotels and strangers' homes when I was in my twenties. No, thirty-two was not old by any means, but there were times, like tonight, when I felt positively ancient.

Maybe Mother was right. Maybe I was working too hard and not balancing it with enough play.

I pulled my hair back from my face, the heavy current of dark brown hair hiding the expanse of skin I suddenly needed to examine. Leaning my head back, I ran my hand up and down my neck. No evidence of jowls or loose skin. No wrinkles down my chest. Tilting my head left and right, I couldn't find any fine lines around my eyes or laugh lines that held my makeup hostage.

Skimming down my torso, my breasts were still where they should be in relation to my waist. My hips were curvier than my mother preferred. Hell, any amount of curve to a female's body was more than a fashion model preferred. But I didn't care. I loved my curves and the way my body moved like a sensual woman.

I let my hair fall back down my back and straightened my spine, jutting my fabulous breasts out and seeing my body in the mirror with a new eye. I wasn't old. I was entering my prime, for God's sake. Hot Italian men were throwing themselves at me and I was turning them down because I had bigger and grander things to focus on. I had dreams, I had goals. And plenty of time to do everything I wanted before labeling myself as old.

Back in my kitchen, I poured a healthy glass of merlot, taking it into my bedroom and repacking, this time with an eye for flair, not sensibility. I wanted to look both professional and unique on camera.

Always be memorable.

Mother meant it about one's self. I leaned more to being memorable because of the flavors in my food. However, a TV audience couldn't taste my food and I would be in Hollywood to judge other people's food, not my own. So I'd fall back to Mother's way of thinking and make sure *I* was memorable. That would drive people to my restaurant where I'd wow them with my food.

Silk nightie.

Tight red dress that made me look like Salma Hayek.

Sky-high shoes to prevent me from looking like a preteen who hadn't hit their growth spurt yet.

Bright red lipstick to highlight the lips that would dish up criticism so sharp those contestants wouldn't know I'd cut them until it was too late.

I was set. Hollywood better get ready.

El Jefe was incoming.

2

—————

ustin

I let out a whistle and instantly regretted it when a couple strolling through the lobby of the hotel turned their heads and gave me the death stare that only the bored rich can give. Jeez, can you blame me, though? This hotel was the fanciest thing I'd ever seen, let alone stayed at. There was a reservation behind that marble desk with my name on it. And here's the kicker: I didn't have to pay for it!

Damn, I wished my sister, Abi, could see it with me. She'd just turned sixteen and would die to stay here and pretend to be all fancy for a few weeks. Instead, she was in a run-down foster home with three other kids in Sacramento, some five hundred miles away.

I rubbed at the heartburn creeping up my esophagus. There was a fifty-ton weight on my chest and a clock ticking in my head. Guilt, for staying at such a fine establishment while Abi was stuck in that hell hole, crept over my body and wouldn't let go.

"Can I help you, sir?" The little guy behind the counter, so prim and proper in his purple suit, had on a polite smile, but I could tell it was fake. I knew I didn't fit in here and he was probably wondering if he'd have to call security to kick me out. He and I had more in common than one would think just looking at us.

I had no idea what I was doing here either.

Dumb luck, I suppose. I barely remembered entering that cooking contest online a few months back. My buddy, Jeb, dared me to do it at the tail end of an afternoon of football and beer—heavy on the beer. I mean, I'd been cooking since I was tall enough to reach the stove, mostly to help Mom out, but then later, because I loved it. I was more of a TV guy, not one to read books, but you could find shelves and shelves of cookbooks in my apartment, dog-eared and splattered with whatever I happened to be making that day.

My friends teased me incessantly, calling me Mr. Martha Stewart. But those fuckers ate every last thing I cooked up, so joke's on them. Anyway, somehow I got a call last week telling me I'd been selected to be one of the contestants on this reality cooking show. The way I figure it, they needed comic relief. Every reality show had to have some nut to get the ratings up and keep people watching week to week. And I was all too happy to be the nut.

Because underneath all the joking and ball busting? I desperately wanted to make a living as a chef. So my grand plan was to distract them all with laughter and then slide right in there with the best damn tasting food they'd ever put in their mouths. That'd shut 'em up real quick. And get me that chef's job I needed to prove I was financially stable and able to adopt my kid sister.

Like Eminem said, I had one shot. One opportunity. I wasn't going to get Mom's spaghetti on anything, but the rest of the song was spot-on. It was go time.

"Sir?"

Oh yeah, check-in desk. I had a tendency to space out recently. Too much on my mind.

"Yeah, checking in. Mr. Cox." I leaned onto the counter and stretched my back. I was a big guy. Fitting into those tiny seats on the airplane was uncomfortable, even for a quick one-hour flight.

Silence drew out and I looked down at the guy's face. One eyebrow was lifted and he was giving me the once-over, more interest than disdain showing in his feminine features all of a sudden.

I dropped my best smile. "Oh, that isn't a cock joke."

He shrugged. "Too bad." Then he clickity-clacked his way across the keyboard of his computer and spat out two room keys and a map of the property. "You're in room 207. Just take the eleva-tors to your right up to the second floor. And enjoy your stay, Mr. Cox." A pursed-lipped cheeky smile and I was all checked in.

I nodded my thanks, gave him an extra wink for good measure, and slid my keys off the counter and into my hand. One duffle bag of jeans and T-shirts was all I brought with me, but I assumed I'd have access to a laundromat or something to keep them fresh for however long I'd be here. I marched over to the elevators, found my room, dumped my bag on the floor, and flopped down on the bed. Traveling was exhausting.

My phone rang from the pocket of my jeans. I fished it out and flipped it open to see my sister's number.

"Hey, Abilene, how goes it?"

"Austin? Did you make it okay? Are you checked in?" My sister's voice came out on a wobble.

"Yeah, I'm here. Just checked in. You okay? You sound worried." I sat up on the bed and scooted to the edge, putting my feet on the floor. If something was wrong, I was prepared to fly back home immediately.

She blew out a sigh. "Yeah, I'm okay. Just got worried is all." She quit talking, but I could hear something muffled.

I squeezed my eyes closed and felt that guilt climb up my spine again. "Hey, you crying?" Dammit, nothing was worse than a female crying. "You don't need to worry about a thing. I'm gonna win this little show, get a nice chunk of change and the fancy job they've promised the winner. The judge will grant me guardianship in no time. You just gotta hang in there, okay?"

She sniffed loudly. "I know. I'll try. It's just I miss Mama too," she wailed.

I scrubbed a hand over my beard and started to pace the tiny hotel room floor. "I know, Abi, I know. I miss her too. But you and me are a team. We're gonna get through this because we're hard-boiled. You hear me?"

If my own eyes misted over hearing her heartache, there wasn't anyone around to confirm nor deny the accusation. I waited until it sounded like she'd gotten the crying under control. We'd had similar conversations quite a bit the last two months since Mom passed away and the state took Abi into foster care. My sister was one tough cookie, but no sixteen-year-old girl should have to lose her mama and her only sibling in the same week. As far as I was concerned, she was due a good cry session or two.

"We're tough Cox, remember?"

She snorted, just like I knew she would. You can't grow up with the last name Cox without knowing when to throw down a well-placed cock joke.

"You should just be thanking your lucky stars Mom named you Abilene and not Waco. Everybody would be pronouncing it Wacko since that describes you better than Abilene."

I could practically hear the eye roll over the phone. "Whatever, Austin. If I'd had a say in it, I would've called you Plano. Never have seen you in something other than those ugly, plain T-shirts of yours."

Now that was a bald-faced lie, but I wasn't going to call her on it. I'd bought and worn a fancy suit just a month ago to Mom's funeral. After we buried her, I'd buried that suit in the back of my closet and swore never to wear it again.

"Nah, the ladies call me Sugar Land." I had a big grin on my face. Teasing my little sister was what I did best. Well, besides cooking.

She busted up laughing. "Ew, I don't want to hear about that. I'm a minor, remember?"

And just like that, I lost the grin and came back down to earth. Yeah, I remembered, alright. She was still a kid and needed her adult brother to get his shit together and get her out of foster care. My part-time bartending gig wasn't going to cut it. It had gotten me through college, but no judge was going to give a twenty-two-year-old bartender custody over a teenage girl.

"Hey, I gotta go. They're calling us down to dinner. Call me tomorrow?"

"Wouldn't miss it. Love you, Abs."

"Love you too, bro." She hung up the phone and I flopped back down on the bed.

Maybe I should have bought some new clothes. You know, to show them I meant business. That I wasn't some hillbilly from a small town pretending to know what he was doing. Yeah, but buy those new clothes with what money? Ten minutes later I was so sick of my sad-sack self I sat back up and brushed off the depressing thoughts.

"Ain't nobody got time for that bullshit..." I muttered. Pulling out my duffle bag, I pawed through my jeans and shirts to get to the ancient laptop that had gotten me all the way through a business degree. I fired her up and found the hotel Wi-Fi. Feeling sorry for myself wasn't how I handled life. When shit got tough, you dug in and found a way out. You worked your ass off until you had what you wanted. So tonight I'd research everything I could find on the three celebrity judges.

The way to a judge's heart was through their stomachs. Wasn't that how the saying went?

My phone rang again, this time the 49ers fight song, a particularly horrendous rendition of a football polka. Every time I heard it, I smiled, because it meant my best friend, Marcos, was calling and also because, you know, it was a football polka. That shit was funny.

"Hey, Marcos, how's it hangin'?"

"Like a horse, my friend. You make it into your fancy hotel without getting kicked out for being underdressed?"

I slapped a hand to my forehead. "What's with everyone badgering me about my clothes? I'll have you know these T-shirts are vintage and hard to find."

He cackled over the phone, not bothering to hide his amusement. When you've known someone since the third grade, you tend to be a little too honest with each other. "Dude, they're hard to find because nobody wants to wear them."

"Hey now—"

"Let me guess. You have your Cheers shirt on right now, don't you?"

I looked down at my chest and saw the word "Cheers" upside down on the faded green cotton. "Yeah, well. Betcha don't know which color, though."

"Green."

I shook my head. "Wow, didn't even hesitate." His laughter picked up volume. "I'm a bit predictable with my clothing. So, shoot me. When you're done laughing at my expense, I need some advice."

He sobered up quickly like a best friend does when a guy goes serious on you. "I know you won't take my style advice, so what can I help with?"

"I've only got my entire future hanging on how I prepare some food the next few days. You've eaten everything I've ever made. The only information I have on the first test is that we have to have a 'signature dish.' What the hell's my signature dish?"

He cackled again and I was getting really sick of how funny he was finding everything. I was all for a good laugh, but I was near full-blown panic-mode. Laughter was unappreciated at the present time.

"I doubt they'd go for hamburgers on the grill, would they? 'Cause you make those all the time." When I groaned, he kept going. "All right now, calm down. Let's see. You make a weirdly good mac 'n cheese. Oh, I know! How about your biscuits and gravy? That shit's the bomb. It even got you laid that one time, remember?"

Okay, maybe a little laughter was okay, because that was pretty funny. Marcos and I had some friends over one day our junior year and one of them brought a girl we hadn't met. She took one bite of my biscuits and gravy and the next thing you know, she was marching me into my room, slamming the door behind her, and ripping her shirt over her head. Who was I to say no to her special way of saying "thank you?"

"I want to win this thing, not get in the judges' pants," I reminded him.

"Hey, you asked for advice. I gave it. Take it or leave it. But what I do want you to hear is how good you are. Dammit, Austin, I've never tasted food as good as what you make with leftover ingredients you found in the fridge."

I rolled my shoulders, feeling awkward hearing him sing my praises. "Thanks, man, but I just hope I don't make a fool of myself in front of thousands of people. I mean, I know I'm only here to be the comedic relief of the show, but I'd still like to surprise them with some level of skill."

"Hey, stop self-deprecating all over yourself, buddy. That's disgusting."

My face scrunched up. My best friend was crazy. "I don't think that means what you think it means."

"I'm no genius like you, but you catch my drift. Stop talking shit about yourself. You're good. You belong there. Focus on doing what you love: cooking."

"Now that's damn good advice. Thanks, man."

"Call me tomorrow and let me know what your schedule looks like."

"You got it. 'Night."

We hung up and I went back to surfing the web, my heart lighter and my confidence higher. No matter how much shit we gave each other, I could count on Marcos to be there for me. And Lord knew I'd been leaning on him quite a bit the last few months. Mom's breast cancer diagnosis came late in the game, meaning she had few options left and only months to tie up loose ends. I'd been there for Abi, and Marcos had been there for me.

I had three really good reasons to want to win this competition: Mom, Abi, and Marcos. Okay, make that four. I couldn't forget me. I wanted to win this sucker for myself too.

"Well, ho-lee-shit..." I was distracted from my internal pep talk by the sight of the most beautiful woman on the planet. Dark hair was severely swept back to showcase cheekbones I wanted to lick my way across. One dark eyebrow was raised just slightly higher than the other, a hint at a fiery disposition that rang all my bells. That and the saucy tilt to her hips had me leaning forward like I could climb through my screen and get my hands on her.

"Damn, she fancy..." I whistled through my teeth.

Then I saw her name: Elle Fierro, Head Judge of Taste Test.

I jumped up off the bed, taking my laptop with me. That model of female perfection was one of the esteemed judges I'd have to impress on the show.

And if I remembered correctly, I had her cookbook. I dug through my duffle bag until I found the two cookbooks I'd brought with me. My tried and true recipes that never failed me. I'd brought them for good luck. To give inspiration when I needed it.

Wouldn't you know it? Right there at the bottom of the one that had a picture of a rustic field with food displayed on the wooden table had "Elle Fierro" typed proudly in some squirrely font only chicks knew about. Her picture wasn't anywhere on the front, back, or inside flap, which was a crying shame.

I'd been eating Elle's delights for years. She'd made me groan with pleasure a thousand times and I never realized what she looked like.

It was almost like she was a recluse with how infrequently I heard about her outside of her two cookbook releases. I'd never seen her in an interview. Or on a talk show. Or pictured in the paper. She could have been eighty years old for all anyone knew about her personally. And come to find out, Elle Fierro was definitely not an old lady.

Well, shit. Now I'd be making my lucky biscuits and gravy for sure.

Not that I wanted in her pants. I mean, I did. But that wasn't why I'd be making biscuits and gravy. It's just that I now had a fifth reason to want to win this thing: to impress the untouchable Elle Fierro.

And if I dreamed of brunettes in tight red dresses with red lips wrapped around... Well, you catch my drift. Don't judge me. I was just nervous about the competition and needed an outlet. I wasn't crushing over one of the judges. I was just overly impressed with her...accomplishments. Yeah.

3

My leg was bobbing up and down like a toddler who had to pee and couldn't wait as I sat for the second hour in a ridiculously uncomfortable chair in makeup. Really, was there any worse way to treat your female stars than to tell them they needed hours of hair and makeup by professionals to even have a chance at looking good enough for television?

Ugh, I hated it. That was another reason I didn't pursue a modeling career back in my teens. Well, that and the fact I needed a step ladder to climb up on to be noticed. You just didn't see five-foot-three models on the runway, and that growth spurt Mother promised would happen vanished as quickly as her last boyfriend.

So, to keep from whining like a toddler too, I went to my happy place. I envisioned all the different dishes I could have made in two hours, sorting through all the varieties in my head and mentally flagging a few for later research. While my restaurant was being built, I also needed to build the menu, the most fun part of the whole thing, but also the most risky. So much of being a breakout success was about public opinion and people's unpredictable whimsy, not the quality of the food presented. The restaurant had to be *trendy* above all else. *Dios ayúdanos.*

"Okay, Ms. Fierro. All done."

The young makeup artist with a bar through her nose finally started packing away her instruments of torture. I leaned forward to gaze at my new self in the mirror, wondering how she Photoshopped me when I wasn't a photograph. I had skin that looked like velvet, without a single pore showing to mark me as human. My eyes were lined with kohl, highlighting the almond shape and deepening my dark chocolate irises. My hair was swept back into an intricate chignon with braids and wisps and approximately a hundred pins digging into my scalp. I wished that were an exaggeration.

My one concession was the lipstick. I'd handed her my signature shade right from the start and told her to work around it. And she had, keeping one part of my appearance I still recognized. I looked like a Spanish princess about to march into war. Even in just my silk robe with black lacy bra and matching thong underneath, I looked fiercely beautiful, ready to plunder villages and rule my kingdom. Maybe two hours wasn't so bad...

I jumped up and thanked her before walking briskly down the hall to find the bathroom. Once that emergency was taken care of, I found the dressing room where I'd stashed my personal items before hitting makeup at five this morning. Getting up at three to shower and dress, then Uber my way to the back lot studio in Burbank for a five in the morning call time was not something I looked forward to for the next few weeks. But sacrifices had to be made and my restaurant was counting on me to create the buzz necessary to make it *the* new trend.

A full rack of dresses from wardrobe were on display in the center of the dressing room. I went through each one, pulling them this way and that to see which would look best on my frame. Though all of them had a certain appeal, I went with the deep crimson dress that wrapped in the front. I wanted my first outfit to be the one everyone remembered. Hanging it on a hook on the wall, I searched through my suitcase.

I pulled out a necklace I brought with me from its velvet pouch, a multi-strand number with large black beads and flat metallic disks. It would drape heavily across the neckline of the dress like a Usekh collar, which was what you'd see worn by an Egyptian. I'd actually bought the necklace while in Egypt several years ago, taking an instant liking to the historical significance. Only the elite Egyptians and deities of old wore a collar like this.

If I wanted to appear fierce, and I did, this dress, the necklace, and the hair and makeup would certainly do it. Dropping my silk robe to the carpet, I was finally ready to put on my armor.

A loud bang echoed through the small dressing room, and I spun around, eyes wide and heart in my throat.

There, standing in the doorway, with his eyes roaming every square inch of me on display, was a large man in jeans and a T-shirt. I stood there stunned, too paralyzed by shock to move or speak. He was good-looking, if a little underdressed. Not that I had much of a leg to stand on with that argument when I was practically naked. Like a comedy movie gone bad, the next few seconds happened with agonizing slow motion.

"*¡Dios mío!*" I whispered. My arms flew up to cover my breasts, finding nipples beaded and on display in the see-through lace cups. I was missing a third arm I desperately wished for at the moment to cover my southern region, but as it was, I couldn't cover everything. At the same time I was trying to cover up, the man's eyes finally flew to my face, maybe remembering I was an actual person, not just breasts and—other things—there for his ogling.

He stumbled back and hit the doorframe, creating another loud bang. Then he tilted off-kilter into the hallway behind him, spinning to hit a member of the crew who was rushing by with a whole cart full of kitchen utensils.

My handsome voyeur hit the cart full speed, doubling over on impact and falling down to the floor. A shower of stainless steel serving dishes, spoons, and a particularly large set of salt and pepper shakers rained down upon the man as punishment for his clumsiness.

I reached down and snatched my robe off the floor, wrapping it around myself and belting it tighter than a corset on a virgin looking for a husband. Marching over to the door, I surveyed the mess and several crew members running over to help.

The chaos gave me a moment to study the man on the floor, staring up at the ceiling like all the answers to the world's problems were located there. He was a big man, but young, maybe early twenties. His jeans were snug and well-worn, along with his ugly T-shirt depicting a place called The Butcher's Tavern. Hopefully their beer was better than their logo design.

His blue eyes blinked repeatedly, but still he didn't move. The crew member who'd been pushing the cart came around to offer his hand and help him up, but he didn't take it. Everyone got quiet, looking around at each other, thinking the guy was hurt. I leaned forward, growing alarmed and wanting to offer assistance like a good human being even though he'd caught me in a compromising position. Just when I got close enough to see he needed a haircut to clean up the messy blond look he had going on, he nearly burst my eardrums with a giant sneeze.

I jolted back and frowned, not caring to catch my death the first day on the job. He thought nothing of it, though, because he sat up and laughed. "Wow, that's some powerful pepper you got there. I'll remember to use it sparingly."

The crew members chuckled uneasily, probably wondering if he had actually hit his head on the way down. Now that he appeared to be okay, my anger at his intrusiveness bubbled back to the surface. I didn't know who this guy was, but I didn't appreciate him barging into my dressing room.

He finally swiveled his head my way and his gaze traveled slowly up my bare legs, over my robe, and finally up to my eyes, having the good sense to look sheepish from where he sat on the dirty carpet.

"I'm sor—"

"I don't care, *tonto del culo*." I held out my palm, blocking my view of his handsome face. I took a step back and gripped the doorknob. "Just stay out." With that parting shot I slammed the door and marched back over to my dress, too agitated to actually get dressed just yet. The sad thing about cursing in Spanish was that the recipient frequently didn't know you were cursing them out. I seemed to have no choice, though; when I was angry, the only thing that came out was Spanish.

Maybe I overreacted. Nerves were certainly kicking in and the poor guy came in at the worst time. Ah well, he was probably just an extra or maybe the catering deliverer. Once I calmed down, I slipped on the dress, the necklace, and four-inch black stilettos. I was ready. Time to make my entrance.

"Each of you will film several shots for the opening credits, then we'll have you film some interviews about your career that we'll splice up and insert as necessary so the viewers know your credentials." Tom James, the infamous reality show director who'd already filmed two other award-winning cooking shows, was going over the directions for the judges when I walked onto the set. "There you are, Ms. Fierro! Wonderful to meet you in person."

The director, a tall, balding man, came over and shook my hand, then spun to introduce me to the other two judges. "This is Bertrand Paul and Michael Fin. Gentlemen, meet Elle Fierro."

The two men stepped forward and I reached to shake their hands. Bertrand, a smaller, older man, squeezed my fingers lightly and kissed the back of my hand before releasing me with a cute smile. Michael, a younger, rugged man—handsome if you liked the outdoorsy type—shook my hand and lingered a little longer than necessary. But if I wasn't taking home hot, rich Italians, I certainly wasn't taking home a colleague. Ah well, he was young. He'd learn soon enough not to mix business with pleasure.

"Let's get you over to your camera man, Elle, now that Bertrand is finished." Tom started to walk off when Bertrand interrupted.

"Oh, I wasn't done. I didn't care for my hair in the first take, so we're going to redo it."

My gaze flicked up to the handful of strands that clung valiantly to his mostly bald head. My eyes darted away quickly, not wanting to make him uncomfortable so soon in our acquaintance. Michael let out a noise he disguised poorly as a cough, which I thought was a little too obvious and gauche, but it didn't seem to faze Bertrand. He found a makeup crew member and proceeded to get all six of his hairs fixed.

Tom rolled his eyes. "Come on, Elle. You'll be fast, I can tell. I'm sure you'll only need one take." He introduced me to the camera person and then moved away, barking orders at the sound crew.

I ran through head shots and short pans, careful to keep a small smile on my face. My natural instinct was to glare into the camera so everyone knew I wasn't the softie of the group, but I also wanted viewers to like me. It was a fine line and I had to be sure to dance right on it if the publicity was going to help me down the line.

The cameraman seemed to be eating it up, so I guessed I struck a good balance. Once I was done, he went back to Bertrand, whose hair looked the exact same as when he did his first run-through. I watched him, fascinated with the way he knew exactly how to hold his head and where to put his hands when he smiled for the camera. He must practice in the mirror quite a bit.

"Interesting character, huh?" Michael sidled up next to me and bumped my shoulder with his elbow, his cologne even more powerful close up.

"Hmm," I answered noncommittally. "I think he'll be a fabulous addition to our panel. When do we meet the contestants?" Better to keep conversation with Michael on a business-only path at all costs.

"Tom said we'd have lunch together a little later and meet them then." He turned fully toward me, his flannel shirt snagging slightly on my necklace he was so close. "You gonna be my buddy during this competition?"

I stepped around him to walk away and glanced back with cold boredom my intended look. "I'm no one's buddy."

I could hear loud chatter as I approached the white tent set up in the back lot outside the Warner Bros Studio where we were busy all morning shooting interview snippets to be used later to break up scenes of the actual competition. A few minutes late to lunch, I picked up my pace the best I could in my stilettos. They looked beautiful on, making my short legs look less stump-like, but damn, were they killer on my feet.

A woman dressed in black outside the tent eyed my badge as I held it up in my hand. There was no way I'd be putting it around my neck and spoiling the statement my necklace was making. Sacrifices had to be made for fashion.

Surprisingly, I was nervous to meet the contestants. We'd be spending quite a bit of time together from what Tom explained earlier today. He'd pair us up for the second challenge, sending us off to a foreign local, so I hoped to get along with all of them. I crossed my fingers not to get some vapid artist who couldn't take constructive criticism or put in the hard work necessary to elevate one's craft.

Ducking my head into the tent, I let my eyes adjust before stepping forward.

"Elle! Come meet the crew." Michael materializes at my side, grabbing my elbow to tug me forward.

Faster than he could say "sexual harassment," I pulled my elbow free and sidestepped, preferring to make my own introductions. The long table was already filled with excited faces, some familiar and many not. I spotted a balding head and went in that direction, figuring it was either Tom or Bertrand.

I came up beside him and asked, "Tom, will you introduce me to our contestants?" He pulled away from the man he was speaking to and walked me farther down the line to where four people were huddled at the last table, looking less jovial than the rest.

"Poor saps have no idea what they're in for..." he whispered out of the side of his mouth right before we reached their group.

I barely heard him as my gaze zeroed in on the largest of the four.

Butcher's Tavern guy. The one who walked in on me half naked.

He was here.

Dios mío, he was one of the contestants.

Everything froze, then lurched forward in slow motion, like the guy was some sort of Matrix character, able to manipulate time whenever I was around him. My stomach clenched like a vise, then dropped to my feet. I felt like I was underwater, trying to flee a situation but unable to move fast enough to outpace disaster.

He glanced up to meet my gaze, then looked away, before darting right back to me, startled surprise, and what a small kernel of me hoped was fear, in his eyes. The noise in the tent faded away as I got lost in his eyes, the ones that had seen far more of me than I ever intended. How the hell was I going to work with him? I planned for every contingency for this opportunity and yet never considered this quagmire.

"*Hijo de puta...*" I muttered, closing my eyes for just a moment. Anything to break that connection. Just a blink of time needed to gather my thoughts and put my armor back on.

"What's that, Elle?" Tom leaned his head down, trying to catch what I was saying down there close to his waist level even with these ridiculous shoes on.

Summoning a smile, I pasted it on my face, certain I looked constipated instead, but it was the best I could do under the circumstances. "Oh nothing, just super excited!"

I wanted to slap my forehead. What a stupid response. I sounded like a damn cheerleader, all exclamations and "like, totally." That wasn't the perception I wanted anyone to have of me. I wanted to be taken seriously, yet here I was mumbling to myself like a crazy person.

And one of the contestants had already seen me naked!

"Well, that's great. I like your enthusiasm. Right here we have Jason Willheimer from New Mexico." Tom patted a small man on the shoulder. He was maybe mid-thirties, wearing a sweater like Mr. Rogers.

He barely flicked his head up and mumbled something that sounded like "hello" in my direction. I gave a tepid smile to the back of his head and wondered how he made it onto the show. He must cook brilliantly to overcome what he lacked in personality. Maybe he saved all of it for his food. I was actually looking forward to seeing what he could create.

Tom cleared his throat and moved on. "And here is Brandy Latrell from Texas. Brandy, this is Ms. Elle Fierro."

A young woman with huge curly black hair and ebony skin twisted around fully and smiled up at me. I instantly liked her.

"Hello, Ms. Fierro, lovely to meet you in person." Her smile was genuine and unlike my ridiculous exclamation earlier, her enthusiasm was real. She exuded happiness and I knew her food creations would be the same.

We shook hands and I couldn't help a returning smile, though mine was tempered by not wanting to show favoritism this early on in the game. "Likewise. I look forward to seeing what you prepare for us."

I could feel a laser-like stare on my face from across the table. The weight of his scrutiny was distracting, though I was determined to act like nothing about this morning fazed me.

"And then of course we have Dale Fitzgerald from North Carolina." Tom pointed to a man across the table. He stood and shook my hand with a beefy grip. The man was overly large, perhaps taste testing more than he was cooking. Or maybe he cooked so well he couldn't help but eat it all. He sat back down and mopped his dripping forehead with a handkerchief. I was looking forward to tasting what he prepared, as long as he could keep his nervous sweat out of the recipe.

"Last, but not least, we have Austin Cox from California." Tom waved in my voyeur's direction and I took a fortifying breath before finally letting my gaze lock with his again. As far as I was concerned, this morning never happened. That was the story I was sticking with.

He stood up and leaned over the table to extend his hand. I reached forward and placed my small hand in his, disturbed when the warm contact sent a shiver down my body. He smiled an easy smile. Good. He was pretending this morning's peep show never happened either.

"Ah, so a local, yes?" I said, surprised when my voice came out a bit more throaty than normal.

The tips of his lips tilted higher, the smile looking natural on his face, despite the beard scruff that threatened to hide it. "Not really. Northern California is nothing like Southern. Technically, we're the same state, but when it comes down to it, we're completely different." His voice held a bit of a twang I wasn't expecting.

"Are you from a small town, then?"

He still hadn't let go of my hand, so I slid it out from his grasp, needing to keep myself away from him. He had a certain magnetism that was disconcerting.

"The show will say I'm from Sacramento, but yes, I'm actually from a small town a few miles outside of there. I'm like a fish outta water 'round here. And where are you from, Ms. Fierro?"

I glanced around the table, remembering there were other people in this conversation. "Originally Spain." Brandy let out an appreciative "ohh..." over that detail. "But I've been in New York so long you could safely say I'm from there."

"Well, that explains your beautiful outfit." Brandy had spun around again and flailed her hands in the air between us. "The dress, the necklace. My goodness, Ms. Fierro, you're a stunning Spanish princess."

I couldn't help but smile at that effusive praise.

"You can say that again..." Austin muttered so quietly I wasn't sure I heard him correctly. I chanced a glance and he was smirking at me, eyes narrowed, like the game had changed and he was remembering exactly what he'd seen in that dressing room this morning.

A blush crept up my neck.

This was going to be awkward.

4

———

ustin

I lay in my bed that night, naked as the day I was born, wondering what to do about my gigantic faux pas. I wasn't super fancy from New York or Spain or something, but even a back-woods guy like myself knew walking in on one of the judges—in a thong—who would determine my fate here was not a good situation.

The salt in the wound was that I was so stunned by the unbe-lievably gorgeous sight before me, I hadn't been able to drink in all the details. One minute I'm opening the door to my dressing room—or so I thought—and the next I'm staring at the most stunning woman to have ever lived. I literally had a split second there where I thought I'd somehow died and gone to heaven. Like the shitty studio was the Pearly Gates and she was some dark angel sent to make my Valhalla a sexual paradise. I may have mixed a few theologies in there, but my brain was permanently scrambled.

Suddenly it was of paramount importance that I remember as much as I could. Like the bare, curvy, smooth legs that led to a string bikini and booty cheeks I wanted to squeeze with my bare hands. Then she'd spun around—thank you, Jesus—and I got the goods from the front. A flash of dark nipples pointed at me before she covered them up, her black lacy thong also sheer enough to show me her impeccable shaving habits.

Believe it or not, all that goodness was not what struck me the most. I know, I know. You think I was blinded by her sexy, almost-naked body like any warm-blooded male. And yes, I was. For a split second only.

Because then I looked up at her face.

And I realized there really was an angel in the room.

Her eyes were open wide with surprise, sparkling with the kind of energy and sass that perked up some twisted part of me that liked a girl with a little edge. Her lips. I was getting hard again just thinking about those pouty lips painted a sinful red. I wanted to hold her face and nibble on those lips, stick my thumb in there and watch her take me inside. Those lips were naughty, made to do wicked things. And I wanted to be the one they devastated.

Shit, now I was fully erect, by myself in my hotel room. I couldn't jerk off to the memory of one of the show's judges, could I? Who was I kidding? I totally could. But should I? My body was saying "hell yes," but my code of ethics was blaring a warning the size of my erection.

It's not like she gave me permission to see her in that state of undress, so really, my untimely arrival was an invasion of her privacy. Whacking off to the memory of that invasion seemed like yet another invasion of her privacy. Which would be wrong.

As much as it pained me—and believe me, it did—I couldn't do that to her. I had a little sister. I was raised by a single mom. That shit didn't fly when I was growing up and it sure as shit wasn't going to fly now that I was an adult making my own decisions.

Just don't tell Marcos. He'd never let me live it down.

So I took another shower—this time ice cold—and then forced my brain to move on to less stimulating things. Like when she'd called me an asshole and told me to stay out of her dressing room. Shit, then I was thinking of her accent and how hot that was to hear her curse in her native language.

That line of thinking wasn't working and there was no way I was taking another cold shower. I mean, I was out of towels to dry off with at this point. It was time to go over my recipes. We were told tomorrow would be the first challenge: cooking and presenting our signature dish. No one would be eliminated this soon, but we were warned first impressions would be huge, so we had to get it right.

I went over every step in my head, thinking of ways to put a new twist on my favorite dish, areas that could trip me up, and ways to get it done to perfection in the one-hour time limit they gave us. I was just about to pull the biscuits, light as a feather, out of the oven, when I drifted off to sleep.

For the second night in a row, I dreamed of a brunette. But this time, I knew exactly what she looked like prancing around giving me my own private striptease.

The bright lights were hotter than I imagined. Add in the heat from the ovens that were already preheated and I wondered if poor Dale might pass out from dehydration before the day was over. I'd never seen a guy sweat as much as him, and I'd been a football player all throughout high school. I wasn't opposed to a good, healthy sweat now and then, but the dude—honest to God —had three full-size bath towels with him. That didn't bode well for me with my station right next to his. I was in the splash zone.

"Okay, we're going to get things started with our beautiful host and then the judges will each say a few words. And then it's go time." Tom was running around the set, getting all the crew and cameras where he wanted them, not even stopping while he hollered directions at us.

"Oh Lordy, I hope I don't burn anything." Brandy was pacing in the small space behind her counter. I was coming to find out she was quite the worrier, that big smile not carrying over into confidence in herself.

"Ha! Do ne wo b th," Jason muttered as he stared down at his counter, moving ingredients around on the granite a millimeter here or there.

I glanced over at Dale for help, but he too was frowning at Jason while he mopped his neck. Guess he hadn't heard what he said either. Christ on a cracker, that guy was hard to understand.

Time to have some fun with this crazy cast of characters. "Did you hear about the Italian chef that died?"

Three pairs of eyes looked up at me in question.

"He pasta way."

Dale rolled his eyes. "Hardy har, funny man."

I shrugged. "I cannoli do so much."

Brandy giggled and I tossed her a grateful look. Someone appreciated my diffusion of the stress around here.

"His recipes are a pizza history."

I heard a snort behind me. Whipping around, I saw the judges were now seated at the head table off to the side of the set. I couldn't tell where the snort came from, but Elle's gaze flicked away from mine as soon as I saw her.

Interesting.

She was wearing a stunning yellow dress, the high collar highlighting her slender neck. Her arms were bare except for a huge stack of gold bangle bracelets up one forearm. The material hugged her breasts before disappearing behind the table. What I wouldn't have given to see her legs right now. See if they were bare. See if she had those tall heels on again. The ones I wanted to see resting on my shoulders.

Goddammit. I had to focus. Not on Elle, but on the competition ahead. I was here to show off my cooking skills, not make a fool out of myself by hitting on the unattainable judge who was so out of my league it was hilarious.

My gaze moved left and I saw Bertrand Paul seated beside Elle, his smart bow tie the same bright yellow as her dress. Thankfully, I suspected he was gay, otherwise I would have been insanely jealous they were close enough to coordinate outfits. A quick glance right and I noticed Michael Fin was checking out Elle with a level of scrutiny that did fire up the jealous beast in my chest. I didn't like the way he looked at her. Like she was a forgone conclusion. A conquest to be boasting about over drinks with his douchebag friends.

I placed one foot over the other and spun back around with purpose to face my fellow contestants, my head pointed straight ahead. I couldn't even see Elle out of my peripheral vision, which was the perfect situation to keep my focus on what mattered: winning this thing and rescuing my sister. My last name was Cox, but that didn't mean I needed to be thinking with my cock.

"Okay! Let's have the contestants ready at your stations. Judges, you're on!" Tom's voice carried over the whole set, thanks to a bullhorn he'd procured at some point.

"Oh, Lordy, here we go. Here. We. Go." Brandy sounded like she might pass out before the camera lights even turned green.

Jason was back to mumbling incoherently and Dale did a final mop-up job to his face and neck before stowing his towel behind his counter where it wouldn't be seen on camera. As for me, I spun back around, but pretended I had blinders on. Ones that specifically kept me from seeing the perfection that was on my left at the judges' table.

The set went silent and the host, Lindsey, introduced the first competition and then sent it over to the judges for their advice and talking points. She had to do that take several times before Tom was happy with it. Then they set the cameras up in front of the judges' panel. They went through quite a few takes there before they were satisfied. It took all the willpower I possessed to not watch Elle's segment like a preteen's first crush. Unfortunately, I could still hear her.

What can I say? That accent got to me. I'd taken the required Spanish classes in both high school and college, but nobody rolled an "r" like a native speaker.

After a full hour of takes, Tom was ready for us to actually do the damn competition. I was already tired of being on my feet and I hadn't even started yet. Surely none of us had any idea it took this amount of work to shoot a cooking show. Damn Hollywood, making it look quick and easy.

The cameras came on and Lindsey welcomed us to our first day of competition. I smiled it up for the camera while my mind was spinning, going over the steps I'd have to take first to make my dish. We'd already filmed introductions yesterday, so all that was left to do was start cooking.

We did that intro scene a couple more times and then it was our big moment.

The buzzer went off and the four of us leapt into motion, scrambling for our ingredients and trying not to do anything embarrassing in front of the cameras. I put everything behind me and focused on making the best damn biscuits and gravy Elle—I mean, *all* the judges—had ever tasted.

I cracked eggs with a flourish, tossing the shells into the garbage from ten feet away, raising my arms up in victory when I scored a basket. Then I was measuring flour, sugar, and baking soda. The blender came out and made a mess when I hit the start button on too high of a speed. Nothing to do but laugh about it since I now had flour all over my Screaming Alchemist Bar & Grill dark navy T-shirt.

It was now time for my special sauce. I fried, then finely

chopped some applewood smoked bacon, adding that into the biscuit dough. I formed each biscuit into the perfect ball shape and put them into a glass pan. As long as the biscuits were light, there wasn't too much to them. The bacon would add a little fun, but the real kicker was the gravy.

So while my flaky buttermilk biscuits were in the oven, it was time to get my gravy started. I sautéed a brown maple sausage the crew had a hard time locating for me yesterday. I'd insisted it was necessary and after calling around to a variety of butchers, they'd found it for me.

Once that was sautéed just right, I drained some excess oil and added butter. Yes, I drained oil and then added butter. Sounded insane, but I swear exchanging the two fats made for a change in the consistency you could feel in your mouth. Then I added flour and then whole milk. Hopefully no one on the judges' panel was on a diet.

The timer on the oven let out a soft ding and I slid out the biscuits that had just a touch of brown on the top. A cameraperson came by and took a close-up of my biscuits and no, that ain't a euphemism.

With five minutes left on the clock, I plated the biscuits and poured the gravy overtop. Lastly, I added some freshly ground pepper. But not too much! I'd found out the hard way the pepper in those grinders was fresh and potent. Which almost tripped me up at the last second as my thoughts drifted to Elle and her fiery disposition after I'd walked in on her. But Austin Cox was no quitter. I'd finish this competition and even if I lost, I'd go out knowing I put my best food forward.

At the final buzzer, I dropped a sprig of sage on each plate, the hint of green giving the dish a refined appearance. I dropped my hand towel and backed away from my counter with my hands raised, palms out. Done. Finito.

The cameras finally stopped filming and crew members filed out to place our dishes on carts. The judges all got Brandy's entree, a Southern fried chicken that looked like something I'd eat a bucket full of and still ask for more.

Brandy stood front and center as the judges each took a fork and knife to her chicken. She wrung her hands and shifted from foot to foot. I'd bet the cameras were eating up her nervousness, knowing it would lead viewers to the edges of their seats.

I almost fell under the Elle Fierro spell, watching those lips chew the chicken carefully, her eyes masking any emotion. I had to physically drag my gaze away and focus on Bertrand. The guy didn't have a poker face at all. If it was bad, you'd know it right away. Michael was animated, but I couldn't look at that fucker for fear he and everyone else would know I hated him. Which really wasn't fair, he'd only looked at Elle the same way I did yesterday. But I knew my intentions. I didn't trust him further than I could throw him.

"All right, Bertrand. Let's hear it. How's that fried chicken of Brandy's?" Lindsey was moving them along, unconcerned with Brandy's nerves.

Bertrand carefully wiped the corners of his mouth before speaking. "The chicken was cooked to perfection. Very juicy and flavorful. The skin was crispy and light. Overall, I'd say that's one of the best pieces of fried chicken I've ever had."

Brandy nearly collapsed with relief, sagging to a bent-over position before straightening back up with her signature broad smile back in place.

I was happy for her. You couldn't help but cheer on such a nice person.

"Ms. Fierro. Did you feel the same way?" Lindsey asked.

Elle inclined her head, her hair in another intricate twist on the back of her head. "It was *delicioso. Muy bien*, Brandy. You have talent I want to taste more of." A soft smile completed her review.

Brandy looked ready to jump up and down.

Michael gave his glowing review and then the crew cleared the plates and replaced them with Jason's dish.

"Your sauce on top of the enchilada was very interesting. A nice spicy top note on a traditional dish. However, the enchilada itself was a bit lacking in originality for me. I think you can do better." Michael grilled Jason and a bundle of nerves started to swirl in my belly.

The other judges had better things to say, though Elle agreed with Michael. Jason mumbled something that sounded like "thank you" and went back to his station looking like a whipped puppy.

Dale was called up next and without his towels to mop up after him, I feared his shirt was turning into a wet T-shirt contest. The judges slowly tasted his barbecue ribs and then gave feedback.

"Hmm...a perfect texture and amount of grill time," Elle said. "Though it was a bit too salty for my taste. A bit more brown sugar would have done the trick."

I nearly swallowed my tongue fighting back a bark of laughter. I just hoped the cameras weren't showing our faces right then. Dear God, the overly sweaty man made a recipe too salty? I barely knew Elle, but I wanted to offer up a toothbrush and mouthwash. Drinking bodily fluids was asking a bit too much of the judges if you asked me.

And then it was my turn.

My biscuits and gravy were placed in front of the judges and I hoped they hadn't cooled off or the gravy hadn't gotten that weird milk skin on top to ruin the whole damn thing. Elle glanced at me quickly before picking up her knife and fork to dig in.

My heart leapt up into my throat and I didn't know if my lungs were still functioning. I got a little light-headed under the bright lights and the examination of the judges. I should have been watching all three of them equally, but I couldn't seem to look away from Elle tasting my food for the first time.

Cooking is an oddly intimate thing. Normally cooking for my loved ones, I ended up putting my heart and soul into everything

I prepared. And here was Elle Fierro, chef extraordinaire and Spanish goddess, putting my food in her gorgeous mouth. Her pink tongue darted out to lick up a drop of gravy that landed on her lush bottom lip. If it couldn't be me she was licking, I was glad it was my gravy.

"What do you think of Austin's down-home cooking, Bertrand?" Lindsey was smiling like time hadn't stopped the minute Elle tasted my biscuits. The show must go on, I guessed.

Bertrand patted his pursed lips with the cloth napkin and spread it carefully on his lap before addressing me. I died a thousand deaths standing there by myself, waiting for his criticism. This was it. The moment everyone found out I was a fraud. A small-town boy pretending he could hack it amongst world-renowned chefs.

"I have no idea what I just ate." Bertrand looked so serious. He wasn't even looking at me. The weight of a thousand future pitying glances sagged my shoulders. I wanted to nod maturely and accept his criticism, but I was frozen. Stunned in my embarrassment.

Then his head swiveled and he leveled his gaze at me, his mouth turning into a smile. "But I *love* it! I want more, more, more!" He smacked his hand down on the table with each repetition.

It took a hot second for his meaning to get through my fog of insecurity. Once it did, I tilted my head up to the ceiling and then nearly doubled over with a relieved laugh. Holy shit, he loved my biscuits and gravy!

"Well then, you keep eating and I'll get some feedback from Elle." Lindsey chuckled and then turned to my next executioner. "Would you agree with Bertrand?"

And that's when things got really interesting.

Because Elle laid those gorgeous dark eyes on me and I saw something new in them. I'd seen her look at me with shock, with angry dismissal, and even worse, bored disinterest. But now? Now there was a level of respect and curiosity that lit those eyes with a fire that spoke right to my soul.

She finally saw me.

"I knew exactly what I was eating"—she gave a side-eye look to Bertrand that was both adorable and cheeky—"but I do agree on his second point. Austin, your dish was everything it should be and so much more. The surprise of the bacon in the biscuits was original and the gravy was perfectly on point. Well done."

The clouds of doubt parted, the sun came out, and with her stamp of approval, I felt like I might actually belong.

5

———————

 lle

Tom gave us a break the next day, allowing for us to sleep in since we'd spent close to sixteen hours filming the first challenge yesterday. I was used to long hours in the kitchen, but filming take after retake was a new form of torture my body wasn't used to. I ran a hot bubble bath in my hotel room, letting the water and the guitar solo station I favored on Spotify seep the stress and strain from my muscles.

I was due at the studio at one to get the directions for challenge number two. Tom had let it slip last night to us judges that we'd be paired up with a contestant even though we were outnumbered. Since no one was to be voted off after the first challenge, the bottom two contestants would have to share a judge as a form of punishment. I wasn't sure who he was punishing with that setup, the judge who drew the short stick or the contestants.

My mind couldn't help but veer off course and remember the way Austin had looked under the lights last night, baring his soul for us to evaluate. I found him to be a different sort of handsome, which I found surprising. He made me feel off-kilter and unsure of myself, a feeling I didn't welcome. I'd come here to advance my own career, and here I was, suddenly faced with the reality that these contestants were here to do the same. That my actions could make or break their dreams.

Finally toweling off, I decided to leave my hair down today since we weren't scheduled to film. Part of me looked forward to seeing Austin again, but I told myself it was just so I could see why I was perseverating on him. I wanted to understand my odd attraction to him when I felt nothing for the perfect Italian boy back in New York.

Austin had a casual air about him, with his worn-in jeans and ridiculous T-shirts. His full sleeve of tattoos looked tough, but his temperament was easygoing. A smile came quickly to his face and I wanted to know how he did that. How did he crack jokes when he should have been scared out of his mind for the first challenge yesterday? It had been beaten into me since birth to take everything seriously and to work my ass off every single day for what I wanted. I just didn't understand such levity in the face of a make-it-or-break-it opportunity.

I was curious. That's all.

Applying the minimum of makeup required—but not without a deep red lip stain—I tossed on a green maxi dress that bared my shoulders. It may have been September, which meant cooler temps in New York, but here in Los Angeles, a strapless dress was perfect for the bright sun. Layering on gold necklaces and slipping into strappy gold sandals completed my casual look and I was out the door.

When security finally let me through to the back studio— damn, they were rigorous with their security checks—I was right on time and slipped into a chair in the back as Tom stood to address the whole crew. I could see a dirty blond head of hair in the front row that had to be Austin.

Not that I was looking for him.

"I just heard from post production. They've gone through the takes from last night and said everything looks good. Congratulations." The crew clapped and I joined in, a bit bewildered. I had no idea what we would have done if they hadn't liked the shots. Would we have had to redo the entire challenge? Tom kept going before I could figure that out. "That means we can move on to challenge number two. I've asked the location manager to join me while I give you your assignments."

A short brunette stood up next to Tom at the front of the studio with a clipboard she referred to as she spoke. "Okay, so we'll have one group in Napa. One in New Mexico. And the final group in Seattle. Specific locations and travel information will be emailed to you this afternoon. Each group will have one location assistant and one cameraperson."

Tom jumped back in. "Pairings are final so don't come whining to me afterward. The whole point of this is to get you out of your normal environment and to learn from local chefs. Your appointed judge will be there to help you at every turn. Listen to them, learn from the local chef, then come back here with a new dish to wow the judges. One contestant *will* be eliminated this round." He gave each of the contestants in the front row a scary look.

My knees bobbed up and down as I sat there listening to everything. I was hoping to get paired with Austin, but the more sensible side of me knew that would be a disaster. Better to get the sweaty man and have a valid reason to keep my distance. A shiver of revulsion ran down my spine at the memory of his sweat-soaked towel from last night. Yep, Dale was the perfect choice for me.

"All right, settle down!" Tom waited for everyone to hush before continuing. "I highly suggest you use the rest of today to bond with your judge and map out a game plan. Without further ado, Dale and Jason. You're going to Seattle with Michael Fin."

Damn, there went my hope for sweaty boy. My heart was pounding. Everyone talked amongst themselves, knowing that meant Dale and Jason were the bottom two contestants.

Tom read from the clipboard. "Brandy. You're going to New Mexico with...let's see here. I can't read that. Oh, wait, yes. You're going to New Mexico with Bertrand Paul."

My nose went numb. I imagined I was drilling holes in the back of Austin's head with my glare alone. "*Hijo de puta,*" I muttered to myself.

"...with Elle Fierro in Napa." I caught the last part of what Tom was saying. Then Austin was spinning around and combing over the faces behind him until his gaze landed on me. He didn't smile, just gave a firm nod and spun back around.

A few minutes later we were dismissed. I stayed where I was, letting everyone mill around while I awaited the inevitable. I'd be spending the next few days with Austin. I almost laughed out loud. Life was a funny bitch.

I felt him beside me before I saw him, which didn't bode well for this trip. I was entirely too aware of him for my own good.

"Ms. Fierro?" His voice was low, the gravelly nature of it resonating with something inside of me. The deference in his tone made me smile.

I turned my head and looked up through my lashes at him. "You've seen me half naked, Mr. Cox. Surely you can call me Elle now."

My inner *puta* sat up and cheered when his cheeks turned red under his beard. But to his credit, he didn't back down. "Then please, call me Austin."

"Oh, but I haven't seen *you* half naked."

He hooked a thumb over his shoulder, his look pure innocence. "We can take care of that right now if you want."

I just smiled at him, not moving to take him up on his outrageous offer. He sighed and sat down next to me, his denim-clad knee bumping mine.

"I wanted to officially apologize for that. I thought it was my dressing room. Otherwise, I would have knocked." He ran a hand through his hair, seeming bigger now that he was right next to me. "Well, I wouldn't have even gone to your room. I just—I want you to know I'm sorry. Truly."

As far as apologies went, it sounded like a good one. Sincere even. I nodded slowly. "Forgiven." I stood up quickly, ready to move on. "Let's go get a late lunch and discuss. I don't lose, which means you can't lose this round. Understood?"

His eyes flashed. With what, I didn't know. But he stood and walked out of the studio with me, his pace matching mine. The silence was awkward with what I hoped and dreaded was attraction thrumming between us. I wondered if it was all in my head or if he felt it too. Not that I'd ever ask. Better to play dumb and pretend it was simply awkward because we were two strangers thrust into an intimate experience.

Without speaking, I went to my parked rental car and he climbed into the passenger seat. We clicked on our seatbelts and I started the car. I could feel him staring at the side of my head.

"You know where you're going?"

I looked over at him completely straight-faced. "Rule number one, rookie. Trust your judge."

The edges of his mouth turned down and he leaned back in his seat. "Okay there, scary pants."

I wrenched the wheel and gave it some gas, squealing the tires as I exited the lot. "Rule number two: don't call me scary pants."

He snorted. "That's a silly rule."

"Yes. So is calling me scary pants." I turned right onto Hollywood Way. "Get out your phone."

"My phone? Why?"

I sliced a glance at him. "Do we need to go over rule number one again?"

"Okay, okay, scar—*Elle*." He lifted his hips and pulled out his phone, awaiting my directions.

"Tell me where I'm going."

His laugh boomed out in the confines of my car. "I thought you knew where you were going?"

I couldn't help the beginnings of a smile creeping onto my face. His laugh was the contagious kind. "I knew how to get out of the lot. Figured you could navigate the rest of the way for me." I shrugged.

He held up his phone. "Not with this thing."

I looked over to see an ancient flip phone in his hand.

"*Mierda*, that's an antique. You do know they make smartphones now, yes?" I swiveled my head left and right, looking for a promising neighborhood where I might find a restaurant.

Austin started drumming his fingers on his knee. "Yeah, I've heard that. Something about an iPhone?" He crinkled up his face, which was oddly endearing. I rolled my eyes at his antics. "Some of us can't afford the new smartphones. Besides, the flip phone works just fine."

A painful dart of something I couldn't name hit me straight in the chest. Who couldn't afford a smartphone these days? I felt bad for him, but pity wouldn't find us a restaurant. "Here." I handed him my clutch. "Grab my phone and pull up the maps."

He paused a second, but when I shook my bag at him, he took it, his hands rougher than I would have expected for a chef. He lifted the flap and pulled out my phone, along with my lipstick. He lifted the tube up and read the bottom. "Rouge Coco," he whispered to himself.

"Hey! Map, please." I turned right down a large street, thinking it looked more promising. His fingering of my lipstick was making my lips tingle. He put the tube back in my clutch and I breathed easier.

"I can't get your phone to turn on." He held it out to me, the phone looking tiny cupped in his massive hand.

I took one hand off the steering wheel and placed my thumb on the home button to unlock the screen. The movement essentially forced us to hold hands for agonizingly long seconds until the screen came to life and I was able to whip my hand back to the wheel. I cleared my throat, ignoring the way my blood pressure seemed to spike from simple human contact.

"Okay, here we go. It looks like if we're the moving blue dot, you can make a left at the next stoplight and there's some little bistro. Sound good?" He was enlarging the map and turning the phone sideways then back upright. I didn't know how he could tell anything moving it around like that, but a bistro sounded perfect.

I made the left and spotted a little outdoor café. Pulling into the parking lot, I hopped out and waited for him at the trunk of the car. He ambled up like he had all the time in the world and no nerves whatsoever being in the same car with me.

"It doesn't go with my outfit." He handed over my clutch, the feminine bag looking ridiculous with his jeans.

I accepted my bag and walked to the front door of the café. "Nothing goes with that outfit..."

"Ouch, Elle. I thought we were here for cooking, not fashion." I heard him behind me, his long strides quickly catching up to me. He opened the café door for me and I swept inside.

"Rule number three—"

"Oh boy..."

I swatted his chest with my clutch. "As I was saying...how you dress and present yourself to the world has a huge effect on your success in the restaurant business. You dress like you just rolled out of bed? You won't be taken seriously. You dress to impress? Doors will open."

"Would you like to sit inside or outside?" the hostess asked with a smile.

"Outside, please." I didn't wait to see if Austin agreed.

As we got settled at a table with the perfect amount of shade and sunshine, Austin had gone quiet on me. I wanted to help him, but perhaps I was too brutal. Wouldn't be the first time I was told I came off a bit too harsh. "Did I offend you?"

He looked up at me from his menu, his eyes a darker shade of blue than I remembered them as being. "I hear what you're saying and while I appreciate the advice and will take it to heart, you need to know I'm not here to become a celebrity chef, or own my own restaurant, or put out a cookbook. I'm here to learn from the best and then get a well-paying job at a restaurant."

I lifted an eyebrow. "I'm confused. Don't you already work at a restaurant?"

He set down his menu and leaned forward a bit. "No. I work as a bartender."

We sat there staring at each other as people bustled around us, oblivious to everything but this conversation. There was more to Austin Cox than I originally thought. How could he have the skill level he'd demonstrated if he had so little experience? I was still just as confused about him as ever. I decided I needed to go back to square one to figure him out.

"All right. Let's start over. Hello, I'm Elle Fierro." I reached across the table with my hand out. His gaze dropped to my hand and then back to my face, his eyes crinkling at the corners.

His lips tilted up and he shook my hand before answering, "Hi, Elle. I'm Austin Cox."

I retrieved my hand and placed my elbows on the table, my chin propped up by my fists. "So, tell me about yourself, Austin."

He sat back and studied me. "Shouldn't we be talking about Napa? What dish we're going to work on?"

I wasn't letting him off the hook that easily. "You seem to think cooking is formulaic. Add this, blend that, bake for a certain amount of time, and voilà! Food genius." I shook my head. "It most certainly doesn't work that way, Austin. Food takes on a life of its own. It's a living thing you're manipulating and changing, then adding in your own unique twist to create something people will love and want to consume for years to come. You can't create food genius until you know the basics and know how to extend from there. Until you know who you are as a chef and what unique twist you bring to the kitchen. I can't help you if I don't know who you are." I sat back in my chair. "So I ask again. Tell me something about yourself, Austin."

"You're a tyrant, you know that, right?" He gave me a wry grin.

"Refer to rule number two."

He faked shock. "Oh, so now I can't call you scary pants *or* a tyrant?"

I sliced my hand through the air. "Enough jokes. Who the hell are you, Austin Cox?" This man could talk for days and not say anything. He had a joke for every occasion. But I wanted to know the real man underneath all his protective humor.

He clenched his jaw and leaned forward. "I'll tell you everything you need to know. I didn't grow up in a fancy place like Spain or New York. I lived with a single mom struggling to do right by her two kids. I learned to cook to help her out and to stay out of trouble. So fancy dishes with French names aren't in my repertoire. I don't have aspirations of being a celebrity chef wearing a fancy bow tie because more than anything, I just want to support myself. I don't need accolades from food critics or cookbook sales to bolster my self-esteem. I just want to do what I love to do and get paid for it."

His hands were fisted on the table, the tension in him obvious. I'd hit on a sensitive subject and I reveled in his passion.

I pointed a burgundy painted fingernail in his face. "*That's* what I wanted to know. Lovely to finally meet you, Austin."

The server came up right then and took our orders, helping to diffuse the situation. When she left, we got down to business and discussed what dishes I had in mind and which chef we'd be meeting in Napa. Austin had good ideas already, yet also seemed open-minded, which was important this early in the game. By the time we finished our late lunch, we had a game plan and the travel itinerary had been emailed to us.

Back in my rental, I grabbed my phone to unlock it and handed it to Austin. He helped us navigate back to the hotel we were all staying at like we did this every day. I felt like we'd reached a truce of some sort. We were friendly, but distant. I didn't ask him any more intrusive questions and he kept the jokes on lockdown. Part of me missed his easy laugh and silly disposition.

I pulled into a parking space and parked, doors unlocking automatically. Austin moved to get out.

"Meet you in the hotel lobby at six tomorrow morning? We can share a ride to the airport." I extended the olive branch, feeling a bit of guilt for being so hard on him. It was simply the only way I knew how to be.

He got out and leaned his head back into the car. "Sounds good. Get a good night's sleep. We've got a competition to win." Then he winked and smiled at me before slamming the door shut.

My insides began to riot, that wink doing damage before I could shut it down. I put the car in reverse and hightailed it out of there, having to navigate for myself without Austin by my side to tell me where to go. I had an errand to run. One I hoped would smooth things over between us.

6

ustin

I don't know what I expected from Elle yesterday, but it wasn't to be interrogated about my personal life. She was a small woman, but she dealt a heavy blow with her cutting words. Those lips of hers, that I still fantasized about like a drug addict, were quick to bark rules at me. But then she'd offered solid advice left and right. I could tell she was trying to help me, but damn, I'd need a Kevlar vest to protect myself from her verbal bullets.

I was down in the hotel lobby at 5:45 in the morning to make sure I was there before Elle. Getting on her bad side so early on this trip wasn't a game plan I intended to follow. I'd thought about her comments as I lay in bed last night and realized I probably should clean up my look. Unfortunately, I didn't bring anything else with me and I didn't have the money to go out and buy new clothes.

That led me to thinking about how she also wanted me to figure out who I was and how I'd bring my own unique spin to the recipes. There was one huge problem with that advice: I was just some hick-town guy with a passion for throwing food together to feed my friends and family. It wasn't exactly a unique story or one that would lead to greatness.

So I did some further research on Elle Fierro last night. Turns out, her mom was a famous international fashion model. Elle had been born in Spain, raised in New York City, and traveled all over the world with her mom. Now *that* was a story! From her clothes, to her handbags, to her choice in Chanel lipstick...Elle screamed money. There was no way she could understand a guy like me with ten worn-out T-shirts to my name.

Which was disappointing on so many levels. The pie-in-the-sky part of me was down in the dumps that we'd never work out as a couple. Not like there was any chance in hell of that happening anyway, but a guy could dream, right? On a more practical level, I was worried I got paired up with the wrong judge for this second challenge. I mean, her lipstick cost more than my shirt, jeans, and shoes combined. If she didn't understand me, how could she possibly help come up with a dish that was both amazingly different and yet still "me"?

"I'm glad you understand rule number four." Elle's voice came from behind me, the slight roll in her Rs making up for the ridiculous early morning hour. Her voice was in direct contrast to her words. It was melodic, her accent thick, despite having grown up in the States. And then there were her words. Cutting. Ruthless. Allowing for no mistakes.

I took in her outfit and makeup as she came up next to me, utterly perfect like she wasn't quite human. "Let me guess. Never make your judge wait?"

She beamed like I passed the first test of the day. "Precisely."

I refrained from rolling my eyes. Barely. Instead, I got busy grabbing my duffle bag off the wood floor and taking her rolling suitcase from her. She started walking out the lobby double doors and I followed behind.

"I thought this trip was only one overnight." When she glanced back at me, I nodded toward her full-sized suitcase.

I could have sworn her cheeks pinked a bit before she bit back in the form of a scathing comment. "Yes. One overnight. Some of us dress to impress, which takes space." She popped open her trunk and pulled out a brown paper gift back. "Speaking of which, I got you something."

She nearly threw it at me and then scrambled to get in the driver's seat of her car, leaving me with the gift bag, her suitcase, and my duffel. Guess I'd be the bellhop on this trip. I stowed the two bags in the trunk and took the gift bag with me to the passenger side of the car.

Sinking down onto the soft leather, I eyed the package like it might explode on me. "Is it safe to open?"

She turned to look at me quickly, confusion in her brown eyes, maybe even a touch of hurt. "Yes, of course. I hope you don't take offense. I just wanted to do something nice."

I nodded, trying to keep the grin off my face. "I know. That's why I'm worried."

She smacked my arm with the back of her hand, the blow pathetic at best. "Just open it, Cox."

"I like how you say Cox..." I mumbled while digging into the tissue paper in the gift bag.

"What was that?" She leaned toward me and I paused to inhale her perfume, sweet and spicy. Not unlike the woman herself.

My hand hit something soft, so I pulled it out and shook it to get it to unravel.

Elle Fierro bought me a shirt. A button-down, collared shirt without a bar logo on the front. It looked expensive.

"Do you like it?" She chewed on her bottom lip as I stared at the dark blue shirt. When I didn't answer, she continued to sell me on it. "I thought the blue would match your eyes."

Ho-lee-shit. Elle was thinking about my eyes. I grinned like a schoolboy finding out his first crush stole his eraser. Buying me a shirt had to mean she liked me, right?

I reached back and grabbed my T-shirt behind my head and pulled it off. I had to get that new bad boy on ASAP.

"*Dios mío...*" Elle muttered next to me.

I got my arms through the sleeves and started on the buttons, my grin growing as I saw that it fit me perfectly, like she'd memorized my size. It felt expensive against my skin, the cloth soft and thick.

Once it was on, I spun to Elle to find her still chewing on that bottom lip. "I love it. Thank you, Elle." Before I could rethink the consequences of hugging the prickliest woman on earth, I leaned over and wrapped my arms around her, pulling her in for a friendly squeeze. I was a hugger. Wasn't everyone a hugger?

I meant to pull back right away, but then the scent of her shampoo hit my nose, and the feel of her warm body in my arms pierced my awareness. She remained rigid, but didn't object, more like she was curious as to what I was doing. Like hugs weren't familiar to her. Which made me want to hang on even longer.

"Rule number five—" she said against my shoulder.

I pulled back and settled in my seat. "Yeah, yeah, don't hug the judge."

She started the car, and with her phone in my hand, I got us to the airport. Once we boarded the plane, Elle pulled out several cookbooks and we spent the quick one-hour flight going over possible recipes to highlight my skills. The idea was to incorporate some food element from our location. In our case, we needed to make sure it involved wine, since that was the predominant thing Napa was known for.

By the time we got to the rental car lot, Elle seemed to have warmed up to me quite a bit. She wasn't overly friendly—I couldn't expect miracles—but she wasn't cold either. We'd struck a good working relationship and my hopes were high that we'd actually pull this thing off.

We pulled into the parking lot of Celadon, its kitchen humming, but not yet open to the public. We had an appointment with the head chef, Samantha Cristoff, to learn how she made her restaurant one of the most sought-after reservations in all of Napa Valley. She welcomed me like she was happy to have me, then she walked me through her main dish for that evening, a Moroccan braised lamb shank.

"Did you ever think you'd be braising a leg of lamb in Napa, Austin?" Samantha asked me with a wide grin while we chopped more garlic. She was a ton of fun and had gone out of her way all morning to make sure I knew exactly what I was doing, not in a condescending way, but like a team player who wanted to see me win.

Our lone cameraperson zoomed in on our conversation, catching the friendly way she bumped my side with her elbow.

"Nah, this was definitely not on my radar. I was thinking more along the lines of a local steakhouse in a small town being the pinnacle of my career."

Samantha shrugged. "Nothing wrong with that either. But from what I've seen, you have skills that go beyond that if that's what you want. I mean, you're the one who came up with the wine reduction idea. If it works, I'm going to steal your idea and take the credit."

I laughed. "Probably shouldn't tell me that when the cameras are rolling."

Samantha laughed right along with me. "Damn! I knew I wouldn't get away with it."

"Okay, let's get back to this reduction. We need to make a few different varieties to determine which one is best." Elle jumped in between the two of us, a serious frown marring her features and tapping on her watch. Wow, back to cold-as-ice Fierro. "We only have two hours left to get this right."

Elle spun back around to grab another bottle of red wine. I saluted behind her back and Samantha snorted out a stifled laugh. Elle spun around and narrowed her eyes at me. "Don't make me go over rule number one again," she snapped.

She brought over the wine and smacked it down on the counter, harder than necessary. I touched her elbow, where the camera couldn't see, pulling her in closer. "Hey, I'm sorry. You're right. We'll get the reduction perfect and win this thing. You'll see."

My whispered apology must have done the trick as her eyes softened and she attempted a smile. "You're on to something here. I just want to see you present something *increíble*."

I squeezed her arm and nodded my understanding before turning back to the stove and getting busy on my second reduction. By the time the remaining two hours were up, we had a perfected recipe and I had a new friend in Chef Cristoff.

She hugged me goodbye after the camera was done filming and her kitchen was humming with staff for the evening meal service. "I wish you all the success, Austin. You're going to do great, I have no doubt."

She had no idea what her vote of confidence meant to me. She then said her goodbye to Elle, a handshake instead of a hug, which struck me as sad.

Elle just didn't know how to loosen up. That was my official diagnosis after spending the day with her. And if there was one thing I was confident in, it was my ability to get people to chill out, feel comfortable, and have a good time.

Elle helped me all day today. Now it was time for me to help her.

Whether she wanted it or not.

When we left Celadon, Elle suggested we stay at the hotel restaurant to grab dinner and finish strategizing. I was dead on my feet and all too happy to relax back at the hotel. On the drive over, Elle was still a little short with me, not enjoying my jokes as I helped her navigate. Not that her not enjoying my jokes was anything new. Dangerously, I'd decided making her laugh was my new mission.

While we were stuck at a red light I started with my most cheesy of jokes. "What if soy milk is just regular milk introducing itself in Spanish?"

She side-eyed me, so I knew she heard me. Her jaw clenched, but not even a hint of a smile. Time to try again.

"What do you call a fake noodle?" Silence was my answer. I was not deterred. "An impasta!"

She took a deep breath, but alas, no laugh. "You're going to just keep going, aren't you?"

I shrugged. "Seemed like a fun idea to get you to laugh."

She gave a dainty snort. "Why don't you save your jokes for your new friend Samantha."

Oh, so that's how it was. "Are you jealous of my new friend?"

She scrunched her face like she smelled a bad mushroom. "Of course not! You can be friends with whomever you like."

"Well, thank you for your permission, Ms. Fierro. For your information, telling jokes and laughing with others is a lovely way to make friends. You should try it sometime."

She wrenched the wheel as we turned into the hotel parking lot. I almost hit my head on the passenger window, which I'm sure was what she was going for.

"I tell jokes all the time. I have plenty of friends." She sniffed.

"Really? Name one."

She threw the car into park and narrowed her eyes at me. "What is your point?" She climbed out of the car without waiting for my answer.

Suddenly, getting her to laugh didn't matter anymore. I was

done trying to be nice to her. I was tired of being dismissed. Some people just couldn't be helped.

I climbed out after her, meeting her at the trunk while she tried unsuccessfully to get her heavy bag out. "That. Right there. That's my point."

She let go of her bag and put her hands on her hips. "What are you talking about?"

I jabbed my finger in the direction of the car. "You asked me a question and then instead of taking half a second to hear my answer, you got out of the car. That's rude, Elle." I started counting off on my fingers. "You're short with everyone. You give out dirty looks like Dale puts out sweat. You bark out rules like I'm some underling who should hold his breath and wait for your next order. You're as prickly as a cactus in the desert. I've tried being nice to you and tried to cajole you out of your perpetual bad mood, but I think it's a lost cause."

I threw my hands in the air and puffed out a breath up to the sky as she stood there glaring at me. "You know what? Never mind. We don't have to like each other. I appreciate your time today and for helping me with that reduction sauce."

I dropped my hands and faced her. She was still staring at me, her eyes flashing as they darted back and forth across my face, but her body remained completely still. A lead weight settled in my stomach and I wondered if I just screwed myself with my outburst. God, she made me so angry sometimes.

Her fists finally left her hips and dangled by her sides. She nodded and looked down at my chest, blinking rapidly. "I'm— sorry." One hand went to her stomach, like the apology had been physically ripped from her. "I didn't mean to be rude. I want your answer. If you'll still give it to me."

Her gaze finally lifted to mine, her eyes shiny with something like remorse. I felt like I'd just kicked a puppy with this uncharacteristic display of emotion. I ran a hand through my hair and sighed again.

"It's okay, Elle. I just—"

Her phone blared out an obnoxious ring tone, cutting into the moment and the truce we were on our way to making. She fumbled with her handbag and pulled out her phone, the one I now knew the password to since I'd used it so much this trip.

"*Lo siento...*" she murmured before answering and turning away, her knuckles turning white as she gripped the phone.

"*Hola, Madre.*"

I hoisted her bag out of the trunk and retrieved my duffle, wanting to give her some space, but also needing to get back to our conversation right before we were interrupted. I felt like we were finally on the cusp of getting along. Not just on a business level, but on a personal level, and for some reason that meant everything.

When the bags were out, I noticed a couple packages of those powder-covered donuts you could get out of the vending machine. Considering she was a world-class chef, it was hard to imagine her finding those tasty. Then again, those little donuts had gotten me through college, so I could kind of understand the obsession. Interesting.

Shutting the trunk, I started to haul our bags into the hotel and check us in when I heard Elle's voice responding to her mother in rapid-fire Spanish. I couldn't possibly keep up with the translation, but her pacing and tone told me everything I needed to know. The bags could wait. I halted right there in the middle of the parking lot and waited for her.

She was quiet for a few seconds, then spat something into the phone before hanging up and gritting her teeth.

"Arghhh..." she let out a half moan, half scream at the moon. She looked so dejected standing there in the dark, howling in frustration.

I left the bags where they were on the pavement, walking over the ten feet to close the gap between us. Without giving two shits about personal space or our tentative working relationship, I wrapped her in a hug, her cheek resting on my chest. I didn't dare breathe for fear she'd push me away, too withdrawn to accept my comfort or friendship.

Then I felt her small arms snake around my waist, her hands resting on my waist awkwardly. If her muscles went any tighter I'd worry she was having a seizure. Above her head, I smiled like a loon. Damn woman didn't even know how to give a hug.

"Seriously? That's all you got?" I chuckled, still holding her tight. She tried to pull back, but I made a noise in the back of my throat and held her closer. "Squeeze me like those little powdered donuts you love so much."

"What—" She tried to pull away again only to have the tight band of my arms pull her back.

"Your secret's safe with me. Come on. Let's work on the hugs. Put your arms all the way around my waist and give it a nice squeeze." She snorted against my chest, but I felt her arms wrap around me fully. In hindsight, I should have thought it through a little better. Once she put some effort into the hug, her breasts—that I knew all too well were perfect—were smashed against my stomach, her whole body aligning with mine and making me realize we were alone in the dark, clinging to each other like two desperate people needing something to hold on to.

"That's much better, don't you think?" My voice came out as a whisper, her ear right by my mouth as I leaned down to bury my nose in her hair. She'd worn it down yesterday and I'd done everything I could to keep my hands from reaching out and grabbing a handful of her thick hair.

Satisfaction of a primal kind hit me square in the gut when her voice came out just as hushed, just as wobbly. "We're breaking rule number five."

"I've never been one to follow a ton of rules," I whispered back.

She digested that and fired back, "But why are you always hugging me?"

"You just look like you could use one. Or several."

She inhaled quickly and I worried again that I pushed too hard. But she stayed. The silence grew out as we stayed locked together, neither of us wanting to end this hug.

Who would have thought a tiny Spanish woman with a sharp tongue and sweet lips would fit perfectly in my arms?

7

———

Elle

I could barely keep my eyes open in makeup that morning after Austin and I took the first flight out back to Burbank. Perhaps if I'd been able to go to sleep at a decent hour the night before, I wouldn't be apologizing to the makeup artist for the several layers of concealer she had to apply to the dark circles under my eyes.

My mind had raced for hours after Austin and I had said good night and gone our separate ways to our hotel rooms. I couldn't admit it to him—*mierda*, I could barely admit it to myself—but I *had* been jealous of his quick and easy friendship with Chef Cristoff. How was he able to make such an instant connection? I'd known Austin a few days longer and here we were bumbling around each other with fights, apologies, and awkward hugs in dark parking lots.

And that's the other thing. In less than twenty-four hours, he'd gotten undressed in front of me and then pulled me into

62

several hugs, whispering sweet things, and completely getting past my defenses.

When he ripped his T-shirt off in the car, I thought I might combust right there on the spot. The man was ripped. I could always tell he was a large guy, what with his T-shirts straining the seams of his sleeves. But to see all that muscle up close and personal gave me hot flashes and intense dreams of more hugs, this time without his shirt between us.

Don't even get me started on the hugs. Who needs hug practice? Hugs were pretty simple, but apparently Austin felt like I didn't give good ones. Which was plain insulting. Although, I hadn't minded the practice...

I shook my head, trying to dislodge these crazy thoughts, but only succeeding in irritating the makeup artist trying to make me look like a well-rested human for today's taping with her magic brushes and powders.

The second challenge would be filmed this afternoon and I was nervous for Austin. Shallow as it may be, originally, I only wanted to help him because, if he lost, it would reflect poorly on me. But now he had to win because I knew what a nice guy he was. He was the underdog, having no professional training to get him this far. That amount of natural talent deserved to stay on this show longer and soak up the training he would receive. Plus, I knew if he left the show now, he couldn't afford classes and it would be a shame to waste such talent.

My change in perspective had nothing whatsoever to do with his award-winning hugs.

"We need you on set in ten!" A crew member stuck her head in the door just long enough to bark her orders, then vanished to go harass someone else.

"Hold on. Just one last..." The makeup artist bit the tip of her tongue while she dusted more highlighter on my face. "That should do it." She leaned back, assessed, and smiled.

"Thank you. I know I was a challenge today." I smiled weakly at her, hoping she wouldn't get friendly and ask what had me stressed. "Off to go get my dress!" I hopped up and escaped to my dressing room quickly, finding the outfit I'd already selected for the day; a long bandage skirt in a deep purple shade, paired with a matching lace fitted top. I wiggled my way into it and paired it with nude stilettos.

I waddled my way to the studio, the tight skirt and the stilettos impeding me. I may have looked a million bucks in this outfit, but I couldn't walk for shit. This was part of why I loathed what my mother did as a fashion model. Fashion designers sold society the lie that this outfit was beautiful, but women couldn't even walk in it, let alone escape if they were attacked. That was a favorite feminist conversation of mine for another time. Right now I had a competition to judge.

My phone pinged in my hand as I sank into the chair behind the judges' table. Looking down, I could see it was my mother trying to get ahold of me again. After last night's conversation, I had no intention of calling her back anytime soon. Once again, she was sticking her nose where it didn't belong.

"Elle, how did your day in Napa go?" Michael sat down next to me, his cologne taking a seat with him. Normally, his presence would irritate me, but today I was thankful for the distraction from my mother, even if it came in the form of a sleazy male. Funny how Austin had actually seen me in a state of undress, and Michael certainly hadn't, yet Michael looked at me with an intensity that made me want to cover myself.

"It went well, as you'll see in just a while. My contestant is going to kill it today." I smiled like a Cheshire cat, playing my part in intimidating the competition.

He guffawed, but didn't comment as Bertrand took the seat on the other side of me. Tom entered the studio and started barking orders through his bullhorn. The contestants filed into the studio next and I was pleased to see Austin in another button-down shirt. Not the one I gave him, but a charcoal gray version that gave him a more professional edge. His hair was carefully gelled today, unlike the messy do he'd sported yesterday when I'd wanted to run my fingers through it to get it to stay put.

When he reached his station, he squinted through the bright lights and sought me out. When he found me, he gave a warm smile and wink before focusing back on the instructions Tom was giving for today's taping. That look, just for me, sent my stomach spiralling. A warmth seeped into my limbs and spread through my body, like an internal blanket, keeping me snugly without anyone able to see what was going on.

"Okay, places, everyone! Five, four, three." Tom counted off two and one silently, and then pointed at Lindsey, who began her introduction for today's challenge. I kept my eyes on her, no matter how much I wanted to veer away and stare at Austin. This was my job. I was on camera. I had to focus.

"So, Elle Fierro. You took Austin to Napa, California. Any secrets from the trip you can tell me?" Lindsey was looking at me like she knew something. The lights were glaring and I felt put on the spot. My mind scrambled, but for the life of me I couldn't figure out what she was asking. All that came to mind was Austin's ripped chest in my little rental car and that fantastic hug. And I'd rather strip down to my La Perla underwear in front of the whole studio than share that.

"Um..."

"Cut!" Tom shouted and Lindsey's broad smile dropped immediately.

"Elle, you have to have a snappier comeback." Tom stalked over to our table, his displeasure with my non-answer clear by the way he was frowning at me. "Lindsey is going to ask you three judges questions about your trip and you need to have something sensational to say. Got it?"

I nodded numbly, not appreciating being reprimanded in front of the whole cast and crew. My face felt like it was on fire.

"Just make something up, darling," Bertrand whispered once Tom walked back behind the cameras.

"Let's try this again," Tom shouted to the studio, then counted in the cameras.

Lindsey started with her question for me, her smile looking a little more forced this time. Thankfully, my brain kicked in and I had an answer I was sure Tom would love.

"Well, let's just say we fully explored the fine wine Napa has to offer. As for specifics, you'll have to see what Austin comes up with." I waggled my eyebrows and went for the smolder.

"Oh my..." Bertrand interjected salaciously. Bless him for helping me out.

Lindsey giggled and kept going, the other judges chiming in with their contestants' progress over the last two days. I finally chanced a glance over at Austin, only to see him looking right at me. I widened my eyes comically, trying to communicate that he needed to look away. The cameras would be wondering why he was staring at me so intently.

And why *was* he staring? His blue eyes were making me feel like the top of my head was floating away. It wasn't a feeling I remembered ever feeling before, nor did I particularly care for it.

"On your marks, get set, GO!" Lindsey's raised voice brought me back to the present, seeing the contestants flying into action creating their dishes while I was off daydreaming like a woman whose entire future didn't rest on her performance on camera.

I needed to get my head back in the game immediately.

Brandy was rolling out some sort of dough already while a pan simmered on the stove. Dale was preparing a fish, which was expected since he'd been in Seattle. I hoped he had some special twist to wow us, otherwise I'd be fairly bored with a simple fish dish. Too expected. Jason had a huge pot on the stove and he was dumping all kinds of things in there, making me think he was making a variety of soup.

And then there was Austin. He was smiling as he worked,

several lamb chops already seasoned and currently being seared in a hot pan. Another small pan was on the back burner, and I knew it held the secret from our Napa trip I should have immediately thought of when Lindsey asked for details: the winning wine reduction sauce.

Celadon had offered us two bottles of wine from their favorite vineyard, which wasn't that remarkable until you looked them up online and saw they retailed for over three hundred dollars per bottle. If that didn't make for a wine reduction sauce that would blow the competition away, then we were screwed.

All four contestants worked diligently while the timer counted down. The other two judges and I were pulled aside for short interviews and opinions on their cooking methods. Lindsey circled the contestants, adding comments for the camera that increased the drama and freaked out the contestants even more.

I tried to stay neutral, but I couldn't help notice that Austin had an interesting way of cooking that drew the eye. The man was positively giddy while he cooked, even when Lindsey was circling his station. That smile of his never left his face and he even cracked a few jokes to break the tension on the set. Being the class clown wouldn't win him this competition, but it would win him friends and even the hearts of the viewers once it aired.

"And time!" Lindsey shouted right as the timer buzzed and the chefs stepped back from their plated dishes.

The butterflies filled my stomach for the first time, the first doubts in Austin's dish piercing my usual calm. I was invested in him, because he was on my team on this challenge and because he'd come to mean something to me on a personal level.

His hugs were powerful.

The first round of plates was brought in front of us. The fish dish from Dale turned out to be a sesame-crusted ahi tuna with shiitake mushrooms, bok choy, and a sriracha aioli sauce. The flavors burst in my mouth and the nerves in my stomach exploded tenfold for Austin. This fish was fabulous and I gave my honest review.

Next up was Jason with his clam chowder. His unique twist was finely chopped bacon—which was a bit of a copycat from Austin's biscuits last challenge if you asked me—smoked clams, and a splash of red wine vinegar. It was quite tasty, but it didn't knock my socks off. The other judges agreed with me, which settled my nerves a bit.

Austin was next, his dish looking gorgeous on the plate. We all dug in and I was beyond pleased to note he'd gotten the reduction down perfectly.

"Oh, now that's good." Bertrand brought his hand up to his mouth in surprise, uncharacteristically crass, by talking around his mouthful. "What is this sauce?"

"It's a fine wine reduction from a tiny vineyard in Napa called Fire Horse," Austin answered, looking as relieved as I felt.

"Aha! So, you *did* have a secret from Napa," Lindsey joked, standing a little closer to Austin than was necessary.

"Well, that winery is no longer a secret. This is incredible. Well done, you two." Michael gave his stamp of approval and my smile grew.

Brandy was last today with her stacked green enchiladas. That dough she was frying up earlier had been handmade fry bread she'd layered with refried black beans and cheese, topped with a roasted green chile sauce and a fried egg to give it that Southwestern flair New Mexico was known for.

We all loved her dish, finding it bursting with flavor, spice, and originality. The nerves were back as I realized she was stacking up to be a contender for Austin.

The contestants were all asked to wait in a soundproof room so we could deliberate and decide who was going home. It didn't take us long to know, but Tom asked us to amp up the drama, so we bantered back and forth to give him the soundbites he wanted.

After getting all the scenes he needed, we called the four back in and Tom had them line up in front of our table. Austin's gaze instantly found mine and while I wanted to give him reassurance that he wouldn't be the one leaving, I knew I couldn't compromise my position like that. I settled for a smile and hoped he knew I'd never smile at him if he was the one leaving. I'd stoically look away and disassociate. But did Austin really know me well enough to read my signals? I doubted it. I'd been pushing him away at every turn. Except that hug.

"Austin?" Lindsey called his name once the cameras were rolling. His head snapped to her and for the first time that day I saw some anxiety in his face.

"You're safe!" Lindsey shouted dramatically.

Austin smiled and nodded, looking a hundred times more relaxed, like his true self.

"Dale?" Lindsey was having too much fun with this. "You're safe!"

I rolled my eyes and hoped the cameras didn't catch it. This was getting silly. Just tell the man he was going home. No need to drag it out artificially like this. I felt bad for him. Both Brandy and Jason stood there looking like they might pass out from the wait.

"Jason?" Lindsey called out again. Then her voice and expression changed. "I'm sorry, but you've been voted to go home."

Brandy nearly fell with relief and I saw Austin pull her into a hug. Damn, he gave those away a lot, I guess. It was hard to smile sympathetically at Jason as he said his goodbyes when I wanted to rip Austin's arm off Brandy's shoulders. Was it too much to ask for a monogamous hugger?

The cameras finally quit rolling and everyone disbursed after Tom gave us instructions to take tomorrow off, get rested, and then return the following day for a dessert challenge like we'd never seen.

I was exhausted from travel the day before and the long day of filming. There were four missed calls from my mother on my cell phone, which didn't bode well for my night. I wasn't looking forward to trying to walk back to my dressing room with my stilettos knifing into my feet, nor the drive back to the hotel. Tomorrow's rest day couldn't come soon enough.

Five weeble-wobble steps into my walk of fashion shame to the dressing room and Austin was by my side.

"Why don't you just take them off?" He scratched at his growing beard.

"What's that?" How could he know what I was thinking?

He gestured toward my feet. "Take the heels off. The cameras are gone and no one's looking. No need to keep up the appearance."

I glanced around and only saw a few crew members darting back and forth cleaning up. Advertising my short stature wasn't something I normally did, but he was right, no one was around to see. I stopped hobbling and put a hand on his arm to steady myself while I bent to take the first one off, then the second.

Instant relief flooded up my legs. I think I might have even moaned because Austin leaned in closer, his eyes darkening in color. "See? Told ya," he whispered. His raspy voice reminded me of the way he sounded during our hug last night. Which of course reminded my breasts how it felt to be pressed up against that wall of muscle he called a chest. The nerves in my stomach from earlier turned to butterflies, threatening to flap around forever unless they got another one of those hugs.

I stepped back and told my butterflies to settle down. Austin and I weren't a team anymore. The second challenge was over. I started walking to my dressing room again, Austin following beside me.

"I was hoping you'd have some advice for me on the dessert challenge. You know, since we killed it together on this last challenge."

I halted, needing him to understand where I stood. Maybe if he took his ready-at-all-times hugs somewhere else, I could focus on what was important. This time, though, I tried to put some warmth in my voice so he wouldn't think I was being unnecessarily cruel.

"Listen, Austin. We're not a team any longer. If I gave you advice now it might be construed as favoritism."

He pulled his head back and seemed to mull that over. "Boy, I don't know, Elle. I bet every contestant left in this thing is talking to their judge right now. I'm not asking you to cook the dessert for me or even give me recipes. I'm only asking for help strategizing."

I put my hand on his strong forearm one last time. "I'm sorry, Austin."

Then I stepped back, ripped my gaze away from his sad, puppy dog eyes, and hightailed it back to my dressing room like the coward I was.

8

———

ustin

I was finding out that with Elle, it was always one step forward, two steps back. Her smile when the cameras were rolling, the way her gaze tracked me as I prepared the lamb chops we'd perfected in Napa, and especially the length of time she'd stayed in my arms last night seemed to all add up to one thing: Elle Fierro liked me. She'd fallen under the spell of my panty-dropping biscuits and gravy.

Okay, fine, she hadn't exactly dropped her panties, but she'd dropped her guard enough to let me in. And something told me she didn't do that with very many people. The fact she felt as soft and cuddly as a plank of wood when I first hugged her kind of gave her away.

But then she'd leaned on me to take off her heels and let out the hottest moan from those red lips and I couldn't help myself. I had to press for more. I guessed we were to the "two steps back" portion of this dance because she'd turned my request for help down flat, saying we weren't a team anymore.

Fuck that. Team Eltin all the way. No, that didn't sound right at all. We weren't your traditional Hollywood couple—and no, it didn't escape my attention we weren't a couple at all—the first name blend wouldn't work for us. We'd go with a last name blend.

Team FieryCox.

Now that's a portmanteau to end all portmanteaus.

All cocks aside, my point was, we were a team, dammit. And she needed to acknowledge that. Yes, that particular challenge was over, but the real challenge was just beginning. I had every intention of getting closer to Elle Fierro and finding out everything there was to know about her. I wanted to know what brand of shampoo she used, who her third grade teacher was, and why she made rules all the damn time to keep people at arm's distance.

So, it made perfect sense to text her as soon as I got back to my hotel room after the taping. We had a day off tomorrow and we'd be spending it together. She just didn't know it yet.

Austin: Brandy's having breakfast with Bertrand tomorrow and Dale is having lunch with Michael. I say we blow the other teams out of the water and spend all day together.

Elle: How did you get my number?

Austin: Really? I held your phone for hours directing you around L.A. and Napa. Of course I stole your number.

Elle: That's quite industrious of you. Are you serious about the others?

Austin: As a heart attack. Save me, teammate.

No responding text came through for several minutes.

"Come on..." I mumbled as I paced my room. She wanted to spend the day with me, I could feel it. Question is, would she let herself?

Elle: Fine. Meet me in the lobby at ten tomorrow. I have an old work associate at The Pie Hole. He said he'll work with us for a few hours.

Austin: Yes! Team FieryCox for the win!

Elle: Oh, hell no. Rule number six: never say that again.

*Austin: *sigh* fine, but I'll be thinking it...*

I tossed my phone on the bed and smiled up at the ceiling, barely restraining myself from throwing a fist in the air in victory. Another day with Elle, another chance to figure her out and get her sold on Team FieryCox.

"*Rrroll* the dough a *lee-tle* bit thinner *thees* time, Mr. Cox."

This chef was going to drive me batty before the day was up. I appreciated Elle bringing me here and everything I was learning about pies. Historically, I was more of a cookie and brownie man, so learning the ins and outs of a new type of dessert was invaluable.

What I didn't like so much was this guy's affected accent. It's like he couldn't decide what country he was from, so he tried out a new accent with every other word. Maybe I was just grumpy because Elle had spent more time on her phone than with me the minute we walked through the bakery door. When I envisioned spending the day with her, I didn't imagine it like this.

"*Lo siento*, Chef Ramsey. What did I miss?" Elle breezed back in, her phone jammed in the back pocket of her jeans. Yes, the woman was wearing jeans. Like they were painted on her, hugging every curve and valley of her gorgeous legs. It wasn't fair. How was I supposed to concentrate when everything she wore reminded me of what she looked like without clothes on?

"He's *rrready* for *zee* show!"

I took a deep breath and kept rolling, trying not to let my grumpiness over this guy's ridiculous affectations douse my good mood. Elle frowned and moved closer, which certainly helped my mood. The chef ran off to put out a fire in another part of the kitchen—literally—the poor girl had gotten a little heavy-handed with the torch while caramelizing the crème brûlée. His sad little whimpers echoing through the bakery made the staff roll their eyes and keep working.

Elle made a sound in the back of her throat. *"No tiene cojones."*

I choked out a laugh, abandoning my pie crust to turn fully into her. I folded my arms across my chest and gave her a lazy smile. "And how do you know he has no balls?"

Her eyes widened. "How do you know what I said?"

I shook my head. "I may not be fluent in Castilian Spanish, but my best friend is. I understand all of your insults and cursing."

She swallowed hard, but didn't look away. "Well, that's quite interesting. So, you know I called you—"

"An asshole? Yes, I heard that, but I figured I deserved it, so I didn't call you on it. I mean, I did just walk in on you naked." I whispered that last part just to make sure no one overheard.

Her cheeks definitely flushed pink. "I was not naked."

I thought of that flimsy material and what it didn't cover. "Close enough."

Her chest rose with a deep inhale. Her eyelids fluttered and she dropped her gaze to my mouth. I leaned in closer and when she didn't back away, I knew I had to think quick if I didn't want this opportunity to float away. I unfolded my arms and put them on her hips, feeling how compact she was and loving every curve I'd never had the pleasure of putting my hands on. With a gentle push I had her walking backward, her eyes still hazy as I leaned in even closer, following her.

Just a few steps behind her and we were in the walk-in cooler. The minute I was inside and no longer visible to the kitchen staff, I closed the distance. And none too soon because Elle started to open those lips, probably to ask why we were currently freezing our asses off in the cooler.

I cut her off, my mouth pressed to her surprised lips. She stayed motionless at the contact and I froze, wondering if I'd just ruined everything. Then her lips moved and I sent up a thousand prayers of thanks and promises of good deeds in repayment for this single moment of heaven.

Her arms snaked around my neck, her breasts once again smashed against my stomach. I pulled her in tighter and teased her lips until she opened wider, granting me access. My tongue flicked against hers and her hand gripped my hair in a tight fist. The pain was immediate and somehow a major turn-on. My head tilted to the side and I plunged in, needing to memorize the way she tasted and take everything she'd give me before she pushed me back. I was desperate for her, all while knowing there would be consequences.

I'd just slid my hands down her hips to grab her backside, my hands squeezing curves I'd seen without clothes, but never imagined I'd get a chance to touch, when a loud slamming noise made us both jump. Our lips unlocked and her eyes widening comically told me our moment was over.

Elle whisked her arms back, folding them over her chest and providing an obvious shield as she stepped back. My hands fell to my sides, empty and cold. And not just because we were in a cooler.

Her lipstick was slightly smeared and, God help me, I couldn't help a smirk from forming, knowing perfect Elle Fierro wasn't so put together right then because of me.

"Quit looking at me like that! We just got locked in the cooler," Elle snapped, the fire back in her eyes, her words whipping me just like I knew they would.

I looked over my shoulder and saw that the walk-in cooler door had indeed shut, locking us inside.

"We better snuggle to keep warm." I waggled my eyebrows at her, which she did not find funny.

"Austin! Be serious. That didn't just happen." There was a

little line between her eyebrows I wanted to touch and smooth out.

Instead, I pulled her arms away from her body and held her hands, ignoring her warning look. "Oh, that happened all right. But don't worry, we can keep it a secret if that makes you feel better. You really think the show would care?"

She shook her head and pulled her hands away to run over her hair, pulling a few strands out of her neat bun. "Austin, it's not about that. It's about me and how I'd be perceived. I have to be a professional. My restaurant depends on it. I can't be cavorting with the contestants."

I lifted my eyebrows, the first ribbon of anger swirling in my chest. "Okay, so let me get this straight. This is about you, not us. And kissing me in private is 'cavorting,' rather than a beautiful moment between two people who care about each other. Did I sum that up correctly?"

Elle sighed, the fight leaving her as evidenced by her shoulders slumping. I didn't think I'd ever seen her without perfect posture. "No. I mean, yes, you summed that up correctly, but no, that's not how I meant it. I just—" She folded her arms again and I hated that she felt the need to put a barrier between us. "Listen, my mother drilled into my head that striving to be the best at whatever you do is expected. Anything less is a failure. She already thinks I'm crazy to love cooking when I'm behind the scenes and hot and sweaty. She's a fashion model, she doesn't understand my passion. But regardless, I'm driven and I have my own goals."

I frowned, hurt that she'd been so blasé about our kiss, yet recognizing that this was the most she'd opened up to me. Ever. If kissing the hell out of her had this effect, I might have to do it more often. Nodding to her, I waved my hand between us, urging her to continue.

She rubbed her hands up and down her arms. I wanted to do that for her, to keep her warm in this cooler I'd locked us into, but I needed her to keep talking more than I wanted to touch her.

"I'd already made a down payment on a space in New York when I got the call to be on Taste Test. It was the big break I'd been looking for. The publicity from this show practically assures my restaurant will be a success. I can't mess this up."

Her eyes were pleading with me to understand. As much as it made me sick to my stomach to agree, I could see why she was backing off. I reached up and thumbed away a small smear of lipstick on the side of her mouth.

"I see what you're saying and I respect that you want good publicity for your restaurant. But I also know I like you. I want to get to know you better. And I think you like me too. Even if you did call me an asshole."

A flutter of a grin was all the encouragement I needed. "So, I'm asking you to see me in secret."

"Austin—" She started to shake her head, but the creaking of the door opening behind me cut her off.

"There you two rascals are!" The chef was back. "I was lookin' for the butter. Whatcha doin' in here?"

I looked back at Elle and widened my eyes. She rolled her lips inward to keep from laughing out loud. Somewhere between putting out a fire and fetching the butter, he'd lost his French accent.

I walked by him to leave the cooler, Elle on my heels. "Just shootin' the shit, partner."

I kept walking, even when I heard Elle snort behind me.

"Annnnddd...done!" Lindsey shouted the end of our third challenge, dessert edition.

I was finding it increasingly hard to focus on what I was doing, knowing Elle was watching me, knowing there were feelings between us that left me highly confused. After our hot kiss in the cooler yesterday, she didn't revert into the closed-off woman she'd been before, but she certainly didn't open up to me any further.

I wasn't friend-zoned exactly. I couldn't describe it or define it. It was some weird in-between land where things went unspoken even when all the signs of attraction were there. Maybe I needed to call Marcos and ask him. I'm sure he'd know the name for it, like ghosting or cat fishing or goat tailing or some such shit.

Somehow I pulled my head out of the clouds long enough to make an all-American apple pie for the day's challenge. Except for my version, I made them individual bite-size pies made with a touch of brandy, each with their own crumbly cinnamon streusel topping. A tiny dollop of hand-churned whipped cream with a sprinkle of fresh cinnamon gave it a camera-worthy presentation. I snuck a look over at Elle, her calm gaze giving nothing away. If she remembered yesterday as clearly as I did, one couldn't tell from her unruffled composure. She acted cool as a cucumber when I knew she was anything but. The girl had fire in her veins, she just had to let it burn free.

"We have a little surprise for our judges before we get started with the taste testing." Lindsey looked all too happy to have a secret no one on the set knew about. "Blindfolds!" She flung multicolored swaths of cloth into the air in a flourish. The judges groaned while I clenched my jaw to keep my lust under wrap. Elle with a blindfold? It was like the director tapped into my personal fantasies to come up with today's surprise.

The makeup crew set about putting the blindfolds on the judges and adjusting hair and makeup before the cameras started rolling again. I tried in vain to look away from Elle, but those ruby lips, with just a black blindfold above, gave me fodder for many lonely nights to come.

Brandy was just as nervous as the first time she stood before the judges, her crème brûlée being the first dessert up for the blind tasting. The caramelized top reminded me of the insane chef yesterday running to put out the fire.

"This is heaven in my mouth." Bertrand was over the moon for her dessert, Elle and Michael agreeing and commenting far longer than they ever had before. Their enthusiasm had me worried. Although, if I was going to lose to Brandy, at least I could feel good about who won. She really was a sweet girl; you couldn't help but want to see her succeed.

Dale was next, his old-fashioned sundae taking on a unique spin with a chocolate stout fudge sauce topping vanilla ice cream and a chocolate Belgium waffle. The judges loved his version of this favorite, saying it was inspired and original.

I was last again, not as confident with my dish since desserts weren't really my thing. Plus, the chef yesterday was more than a little crazy. I wondered if he really taught me anything or if he just liked to practice his accents by talking out loud. Elle had said he knew his stuff when it came to pies, so I'd refer to rule number one and trust my judge.

Before the judges could take a bite, I held my hands up silently to stop Lindsey from instructing them to eat and approached the judges' table. Since my dessert was bite-sized, I had a harebrained idea that wouldn't leave once it was in my head. My only excuse was that I was young and driven by testosterone and not actual brain cells.

I picked up one small apple pie bite and held it between my thumb and index finger. I brought it up to Elle's mouth and grazed it across her bottom lip. She pulled back a fraction of an inch in surprise before smiling and opening her mouth.

All the blood in my body headed south and I hoped my excitement was covered by the table at waist height. I placed the dessert in her mouth and watched her lips close around it. I'd never seen anything more sensual than Elle eating my dessert from my fingers.

At the last second—way too late to be helpful—the one brain

cell actually functioning in this scenario screamed at me to stop what I was doing. Everyone in the studio would know I had a thing for her now. And that was exactly what she didn't want. She'd be pissed and never talk to me again.

So, I slid my thumb across her lips and down her chin, spreading the dessert on her flawless skin like a groom at his wedding when the cake-smash portion of the ceremony commenced. The contestants and crew laughed, and the sexual tension was diffused.

Out of nowhere, something slammed down on my wrist, my hand only an inch or so away from Elle's face in retreat. I looked down to see that it was Elle's hand holding me in a vise grip. She held me there, clearly angry and not at all happy I'd smeared her with food on television, for all to see.

I lifted my eyebrows in mock terror. After a few moments she let me go and I crept back to my station. There was no way she didn't know it was me. I knew she liked to look put together. She was religious about it, almost as concerned about it as she was of her reputation in general. So she was going to be pissed.

The only question was, how pissed?

9

———

lle

Eyes were said to be the windows to the soul. Austin should've counted himself lucky that my eyes were covered up by that ridiculous blindfold. Because if he'd looked into my eyes when he smeared his dessert across my face, he would've seen a raging inferno about to swallow him up, burn him to a crisp, and spit him out as charcoaled ash.

I'd never been so angry in my life. Not even at my mother, and she had sorely tested me over my thirty-two years. I'd just explained to Austin the day before that keeping my reputation spotless was everything to me. Even if he didn't agree, or simply didn't understand the importance, didn't mean he should purposely jeopardize that for me.

I was livid.

"I'm sorry to say, the contestant being voted off today is...." Lindsey drew out the announcement, adding drama that Tom ate up like little kids with buckets of chocolate on Halloween night. "...Dale Fitzgerald!"

The remaining contestants all stared at each other in bewilderment. Even the cast gave an auditory gasp at the announcement. Everyone thought Austin should be going home. And if I'd had anything to do with it, he would have.

I'd lobbied for him to be sent home when we huddled up to deliberate, but Bertrand and Michael felt he was progressing, so well, they wanted to see what he'd make next. Then Tom had poked his head in and basically threatened us not to send Austin home since he firmly believed Austin would single-handedly raise ratings with his antics and good looks.

That only added fuel to the fire burning in my gut. Telling us we had to keep Austin here was like waving a red flag in front of a bull. But like the professional I damn well was, I slapped on a smile, squared my shoulders, and walked back onto the set to do my job.

The cameras finally quit rolling when Tom was assured he got all the shots he needed for the episode. I threw caution to the wind and practically ran to my dressing room, my platform heels be damned. If I didn't get out of there immediately, I was going to explode.

I was practically vibrating with anger as I sat in my chair, alone in the dark room, coming to terms with what just happened out there. What bothered me the most was that for a brief second, I'd enjoyed Austin's fingers in my mouth. It was so hot, I'd felt the room tilt and my belly dip like I'd taken a ride on a roller coaster. I'd lost control of my emotions in front of my colleagues and, soon, in front of a television audience.

That wasn't like me, which made Austin dangerous. He had some sort of control over my libido, his finger right on the pulse point, able to turn me off and on at his whim. I'd been right to back off yesterday and shut it down. Or try to, at least.

I was actually surprised he wasn't banging down my door

right then, begging me to give him a chance. I'd made myself perfectly clear yesterday and he gave me space, which led me to falsely believe he'd given up. If today's little demonstration was any indication, he hadn't given up at all, rather just regrouped.

I sighed and stood up to take off my dress, the anger still there but on a low simmer now. My temper ran hot, zero to sixty in a split second, but it also cooled off nearly as quick. I'd have to talk to Austin and explain that his stunt in front of everyone was unacceptable and couldn't happen again. But that time wasn't right now. A hot bath and glass of merlot sounded like what I needed.

Overnight a late summer storm had blown in, the wind whipping the rain against the windows in my hotel room and keeping me up half the night. I still got up early and meticulously got myself ready. Today was the start of the filming for the fourth challenge. I was a bit doubtful of that happening, given the weather. Tom had insinuated that today's filming would involve the great outdoors. Which was currently spitting rain like my uncle Arturo when his dentures didn't fit right.

I ran downstairs and saw Austin and Brandy chatting in the lobby while they waited for the valet to bring their rental cars. My intention was to sweep right by, but Austin snaked his arm out and pulled me into their conversation. He was smart enough to let go of my arm and keep his attention mostly on Brandy. My anger may have cooled a few degrees overnight, but it wasn't gone.

"Congratulations to you both on being the last contestants standing." I forced my cheeks to pull my lips apart in some semblance of a smile.

"Thanks!" Brandy was her bubbly self, oblivious to the black cloud hanging over my head and all over Los Angeles County this morning.

"Wanna catch a ride with me? No use taking two cars." Austin spoke carefully, his smile set in place, appearing casual to anyone looking. But I knew his eyes. They were a darker blue this morning, a look of determination that wasn't normally there with his easygoing manner.

"Sure." That would be a perfect time to tell him where things stood. Private. Only a short time together before we had to get to the set.

By the time Brandy got in her car and we climbed into Austin's, I had a planned speech ready to go, the calm smile frozen on my face to keep up appearances should anyone see us leaving the hotel together.

The minute his door slammed shut and we were alone, I spun to him and launched in. "I don't know what you—"

"I'm so sorry."

His gentle apology washed over my tirade and I fell silent. His eyes spoke more than his lips. They were soft and sincere. What little I had left of my rage was doused by his simple and heartfelt apology.

I sighed. "Austin."

He put his hand on my arm and leaned closer, not in a suggestive way, but in a "please listen to me" kind of way. "I know. I'm so damn sorry for what I did. All of it. Feeding you, possibly exposing anything about our feelings, smearing the food on your face." He scrubbed a hand over his face. "I don't know what I was thinking. Hell, I wasn't thinking at all. That's the problem. I just saw you in that blindfold and I had to touch you."

His tortured expression melted the hardness I'd built up against him since the taping. That yearning, that desperate pull he described was achingly familiar. I felt it and fought it every time I saw him, heard him, or thought about him.

Being this close, I wondered why I fought it. His blue eyes and unruly hair made all the reasons fade away. The memory of his warm hugs and even hotter kiss ate away at my solid professional reasons for denying what we both wanted.

"Austin."

He leaned even closer, eyelids drooping. "You keep saying my name like that and I won't be able to keep my hands off you, Elle."

"I don't know that I want you to keep them off me," I whispered back.

A loud car horn broke us apart, both of us completely unaware that we hadn't left the hotel. Austin's car was blocking the flow of cars trying to get in and out.

His laugh echoed in the confined space as he put it in gear and pulled out of the parking lot. "Let's push pause on that, huh?"

The weather was cold and dreary out, but it felt like a thousand degrees in that car. I couldn't believe I'd gone from wanting to rip him a new one to almost kissing him in full sight of anyone in the hotel.

"Definitely need a pause button. You're giving me hot flashes."

He barked out a laugh that made the edges of my mouth turn up despite myself. "You're a little too young to be getting hot flashes, Ms. Fierro."

"Hmm...I wouldn't say that..." I shook my head and looked out the window at all the traffic. The minute the sky spat rain Los Angeles drivers lost their minds and couldn't drive, gridlocking every intersection all over town.

"Wait, how old *are* you?" Austin looked over at me quickly, his eyes growing.

"How old do you think I am?"

"Oh, I don't think so, lady. I'm not stepping into that quagmire."

"Quagmire?"

"Yeah, you know. When a woman asks if her new pants make her ass look big. Or a beautiful woman like yourself asks how old

I think she is. There is never a good answer. Ever. I refuse to play that game."

I blinked. I loved his honesty.

"That's probably a good strategy. I'm thirty-two, by the way." I shrugged. "Wouldn't want you stuck in a quagmire." God, the man made me laugh, throwing out weird words and being afraid of offending me somehow. I mean, he'd been pissing me off left and right since I met him and only *now* was he worried about that?

I realized belatedly that there was silence in the car, so I looked back over to see his jaw dropped.

"What?"

"You're thirty-two? Seriously?" Now he had a big grin on his face.

"Yes. What's so funny about that?" I crossed my arms over my chest.

"I got myself a cougar, that's what's funny." Austin was back to laughing, the expression so natural I wondered if he came into this world with a laugh and a smile. Then his meaning registered and I slapped my hand down on his arm, the one on the gear shifter.

"Wait, how old are *you*?"

He glanced over and then broke out laughing again.

"Austin!" I gripped his forearm, admiring its girth, but trying to remain focused on getting him to answer.

"Ouch, woman! I'm twenty-two." He pretended to shake off my hand, then grabbed it and laced our fingers together, placing our joined hands on his thigh.

I couldn't focus. We were holding hands and it felt so foreign, yet so good. I'd dated plenty in my thirty-two years, but never in long-term relationships where hand holding became a thing. It was intimate, somehow, having a part of my body tangled with his. It made me think of other ways our bodies could be tangled together.

All too soon, he pulled into the parking lot of the location we'd been given for today's shoot. It looked to be a cute park with a large expanse of grass and tall trees dotting the land. The rain and overcast skies made everything appear dreary and unwelcoming.

Austin brought our hands to his mouth, kissing my hand and each finger before releasing me and climbing out of the car.

I took a few deep breaths and willed away the desire that had bloomed in my belly despite my best efforts to nip it in the bud. Austin was only twenty-two. Barely a man in numbers, but making an impression no man my own age had ever made. And I wasn't sure how I felt about that.

Tom shouted to be heard over the pouring rain hitting the porch roof of the public bathrooms we were all huddled under. "Obviously, this isn't ideal for an outdoor shoot. We're going to suspend filming until the rain subsides. At this point, even if it lets up in an hour, we won't have enough light to finish the challenge, so we're back here tomorrow. Everybody, enjoy your day off!"

A collective shout of joy went up from the group as we all dashed back to our cars with big umbrellas. I, for one, was looking forward to being back in the car with Austin. I couldn't wrap my brain around his age. I'd always dated older men, so to even be interested in one so young had me discombobulated.

He was literally all wrong for me.

We sat in charged silence as the rain pitter-pattered on the metal roof of his car. The rest of the crew drove away and still we stayed. Staring into his eyes was like going down the rabbit hole; no rational thought could stay in my head to remind me why this was a bad idea. I could literally feel my brain turning to mush and my body taking over the reins, directing me right into Austin's arms.

His hand crept over to my side, finding my thigh and squeezing. The sight of his big hand on my leg sent shivers up my spine. What could those hands do to the rest of me?

"Let's go get some breakfast, huh?" Austin whispered finally.

I nodded, too afraid to open my mouth and speak lest I invite him straight to my room instead.

He started the car and drove, my gaze never leaving his face, or his broad chest in a black Henley, or his muscular thighs in his dark wash jeans worn down in all the right spots, or his hand on my leg. With my finger I traced a vein from the back of his hand, over his wrist, and up his arm until it disappeared into his sleeve pushed up to just below his elbow. I wanted to see where it went without the damn shirt in the way.

"Elle..." My name, a deep rumble from his chest, was the most delicious thing I'd ever heard.

"Austin," I whispered back, my finger abandoning his vein and playing with the fine hairs on his arm, fascinated with the different color of his skin and the way his hands were rough on the fingertips and knuckles.

"How about room service?" He looked over, one eyebrow raised, a desperate hope showing in his eyes, a mirror to what I felt inside.

I hung there on the precipice, debating, deliberating, and finally realizing that the choice was already made. I'd go anywhere with Austin. I hoped it was just an itch I needed to scratch, and once I did, I could move on and get him out from under my skin. There was no other outcome. This thing between us came with a built-in expiration date. When filming ended, I went back to my life on the East Coast, and he was staying here in California. That thought pushed me to speak, wanting to take advantage of the time we had left.

"Yeah, that sounds perfect." A smile crept onto my face and wouldn't leave the entire rest of the way to the hotel. He'd already had an effect on me, spreading smiles like the norovirus in winter.

When we pulled into the hotel parking lot, he spoke again, his voice low, almost like he thought speaking too much or too loudly would break some kind of spell I was under. Little did he know I wanted this as badly as he did.

"My room?" he whispered.

I nodded and grabbed my purse, silencing my phone. I stepped out of the car and walked to the hotel without a backward glance, knowing he'd follow. Every inch of me wanted to be next to him, pressed up against his side, letting his warmth envelop me while the rain steamed off of us. But that would be career suicide to be seen together in that way and I wasn't that far gone. I'd never be that far gone.

Team FieryCox would remain a secret.

I choked back a giggle. This was insane. He was insane. And in just a little bit, we'd be insane together.

The elevator ride to Austin's room on the fifth floor was straight torture with us two feet apart and vibrating with sexual need. An old lady got on the elevator and gave us a weird look as she exited two floors down from Austin's room. I understood her look. You could have cut the tension with a knife.

Austin fumbled in his pocket for his room card key, flashing it quickly when we reached his door and getting the damn thing open before practically pushing me inside. His room looked just like mine, except far neater with nothing left out on the desk or dresser. The bed wasn't made yet as housekeeping hadn't come around that early in the day.

That was the last cataloguing of his room I got before Austin's hands were in my hair and his mouth was on mine. The kiss was desperate, our lips and teeth trying to devour the other before this moment disappeared. My hands ripped his shirt out of the waistline of his jeans, climbing up his back and feeling that expanse of muscle and warm skin.

He made a noise in the back of his throat and then his hands were gone from my hair, spinning me around and yanking on the zipper to my dress. He slid the wide straps over my shoulders and the dress fell to the floor in a heap at my feet.

"Hmm..." His appreciative groan torqued the fire in my core higher. The last time he'd seen me like this was the first day I'd met him. I was having a much different reaction today. I wanted him to see every inch of me.

He dropped down to his knees and I gasped, not understanding what he was doing. Then his hands slid down my thighs, over my calves, and to my feet. His thick fingers worked on the tiny buckles of my wedges until he got them off my feet and threw them somewhere over his shoulder.

He glided a rough palm over my thigh and then pressed a kiss there before continuing on the other thigh. My stomach was next, tightening with his ministrations, finding the brush of his beard especially sensitive there. He stood up fully, towering over me without my heels to overstate my height.

As much as I loved him touching me, I wanted to do the same to him. We'd already been in this scenario once before with me barely dressed and him fully clothed. This time, I wanted to see *him*. Yanking his T-shirt up, he took over for me and pulled it over his head and threw it by my shoes.

Finally.

I got to ogle his chest openly. Heat pooled low in my stomach as I saw just how big Austin was up close and personal. His chest was massive, a fine sprinkling of hair leading down to blocks of abdominal muscles I traced with my finger. My touch caused goose bumps to rise on his skin, heightening my own desire. Austin had gone still, so I kept going, dragging my fingers down the patch of hair that dropped out of sight into the waistband of his jeans.

I popped the button and slid the zipper down, already feeling a bulge straining to be freed from its confines. Now that I'd taken my foot off the brake, I wanted to push on the gas pedal, so I dipped my hand into his boxers and found more than a handful waiting for me. His cock was long and hard and hot, my fingers unable to meet when I wrapped my hand around it.

He made a strangled noise above me, his hand closing around mine and holding me still.

"Wait," he rasped.

He pushed his jeans and boxers down, stepping out of them, but still, I didn't let go. I finally had my hands on the gear stick and I was ready to go full speed ahead.

10

She was squeezing the life out of me and I didn't know if I liked it or if I was going to die from the pressure. I was learning there was nothing mediocre about Elle. She was either hot or cold. Ice or fire. And thankfully, she was an inferno of flames in my arms right now, gripping my cock like it was the lifeline she'd been waiting for.

I walked her backward toward my bed, following her down when the back of her legs hit the bed and she tumbled back. Pulling her hand from my cock, I extended both her arms above her head where they wouldn't keep grabbing me and threatening to end this thing much earlier than I had any intention of.

Now I had her under me, at my mercy, her eyes glazed over. Her white teeth bit into her lower lip and I wanted to tug it free and claim those lips as mine now. I'd been daydreaming about those lips from the second I saw her picture online before Taste Test started filming.

Instead, I explored, flicking open her bra to free the most gorgeous breasts I'd ever had the pleasure to see. Lucky me, I'd get to touch them and taste them too.

"Don't move those hands."

Her eyes narrowed at my command, but she obeyed. "Quite bossy for a young thing," she whispered back.

I smirked, enjoying that even now, with her hands above her head and my face between her breasts, she could throw sass at me with such confidence. "Just you wait, I haven't even started yet, old lady."

She sucked in a deep breath, her breasts rising, like they were offering themselves up to me. I accepted their lovely invitation and took one beaded nipple in my mouth, my tongue, lips, and teeth feasting on her body until she was writhing underneath me, her mouth blessedly silent.

Elle's hands pushed hard on my chest, popping her nipple out of my mouth with a loud pop as I jerked back. She hooked her thumbs in the sides of her thong, wiggling them down her legs. I finished the job for her and then grabbed behind her knees, dragging her abruptly to the edge of the bed. Her legs had nowhere to rest except for on my shoulders as I knelt by the bed.

I dipped my head and inhaled her scent, my hot breath coaxing a long, strangled moan out of her. Then I went to work, eating out my chef like she was the day's special. I'd skipped ahead to dessert, finding her everything I'd dreamed of and more. She started shouting words I didn't recognize, Spanish phrases my buddy Marcos had never used. All I cared about was bringing her pleasure over and over again before she left my bed. And if the hands yanking on my hair were any measure, I was succeeding.

Her thighs contracted around my head, holding me to her center, my fingers inside her and my tongue lapping her up. I could feel her convulsing from the inside, an experience I would commit to memory forever. When her legs flopped to the sides, boneless and spent, I climbed back up her body, claiming those red lips again, making sure they remembered me, their new owner. No, wait, I had that backward. They were the master, while I was merely an unworthy worshipper.

"*Vamos a joder*," she whispered against my mouth.

I stilled, translating and trying to respond in kind. "No. *Hagamos el amor.*"

Her eyes flew open and she stared at me, her defenses struggling to relent. We wouldn't be fucking as she suggested. This would be making love. The difference was everything. I tilted my hips, the tip of my cock dragging through her folds and making those eyes flutter with want. It was a shameless play for her agreement. I wasn't too proud to blackmail.

She nodded, which was probably the only green light I could hope for. I leaned away from her and felt around the floor for my duffle bag. Thankfully, I'd had the foresight to bring a package of condoms on this trip. I thanked my young, optimistic self and grabbed one, ripping it open and rolling it on as quickly as I could.

As soon as that was taken care of, I settled back between Elle's thighs. I nuzzled against her neck and looked her in the eye. "Are you sure?" I asked like the biggest dumbass on earth.

"Rule number one, Austin." She smiled coyly and I nearly came on the spot. Fuck yes, I'd trust my chef. I'd trust her to receive my cock and the pounding it was about to give her.

I slid inside, inch by agonizing inch, giving her time to adjust, even though my legs were shaking from having to hold back. She was a foot shorter than me and tiny. I didn't mean to brag, but Chris Pine said it best when he admitted he was above average. When she lifted her hips, I took that as permission to thrust. And thrust I did.

Repeatedly.

Until she was bucking under me and thrashing her head back and forth on my comforter. Her eyes squeezed shut and she screamed my name. I memorized the way she looked with a sheen of sweat covering her perfect skin, cheeks flushed, hair a wild mess, and her face a mask of ecstasy that I alone had given her.

One last thrust and I was following after her, the pleasure clearing my brain and locking every muscle into a charley horse of epic proportions. I collapsed on top of her, aware I was probably crushing her, but unable to do anything about it just then.

A poke to my side had the room coming back to me, my awareness creeping in after the best orgasm I'd ever had.

"Can't breathe down here, Cox-man," Elle teased me.

I smiled into her hair and lifted up onto my elbows, my arms bracketing her face. "Told you Team FieryCox was a winner."

She rolled her eyes and I rolled off her lush body. A quick trip to the bathroom and I was back, pleased to see her under the sheets, hogging my pillow. For a second there, I was afraid she'd dart back to her room the minute I turned my back.

I slid in next to her and moved her over, tucking her into my side and running my hands over her hip, unable to stop touching her. It was a bit surreal to see her naked in my bed, her pristine lipstick gone, smudged by my own mouth. I liked the look of those red painted lips, but I was also finding her naked lips appealing, knowing I was one of only a handful to see her that way.

Her hand slid from my chest down to my cock, already on his side and asleep for the night. I wasn't ready.

"Hey!" I nearly dislodged her head from my chest in my surprise.

She laughed. Actually laughed at me, which didn't help the problem any, let me tell you. Then she climbed over my body, straddling my hips and planting her fists in the pillows on either side of my head.

"Oh, and you called *me* the old lady, huh? I'm ready to go for round two already."

Her breasts were right in my face and my hands itched to hold their weight, so I went for it. Her eyes widened as she felt instant movement under her hips.

"Just keep talking your sass, lady, and I'll be ready again before you know it. You're lucky I find your mouth a total turn-on." Playful Elle was turning out to be my favorite person ever.

"You know what I want?" She raised her dark eyebrow at me. More movement.

"My cock?"

Another eye roll. "I want you to call me by my nickname."

I cocked my head. "What's your nickname, sweetheart?"

"El Jefe. The Boss."

I threw back my head and laughed, momentarily forgetting about the breasts that filled my hands. "That is too perfect." I sobered quickly and lifted my head to take a nipple into my mouth as apology for taking my mind off them for even a second. She moaned and gave me more, her other breast now resting on the side of my face. I could have happily died right there, choked to death by Elle Fierro's magnificent breasts.

Releasing them regretfully, I swept her hair back where it was hanging over us and pulled her in for a kiss. When her eyes went fuzzy and her mouth went quiet, I whispered, "I'll call you El Jefe, but I'll be the one to boss you around. Deal?"

Her eyes crinkled in the corners and she looked all too happy to let me rule her body.

"Get off me and stand by the dresser." I didn't know if she'd actually do it, but I had to find out. She licked her lips and I could almost see her brain working through it, trying to decide if she'd relinquish control. My answer was her pushing off my chest and scrambling to get off the bed.

She walked slowly to the dresser, her hips swinging as she put on a show for me. Stopping at the dresser, she looked back at me over her shoulder, biting her lip. I sat up, my gaze never leaving that lip that brought me to my knees. I prowled more than walked my way over to her, my cock fully loaded and ready to engage. My duffel bag was still on the floor by the bed, the package of condoms right there for me to easily snag a few on my way.

I approached her from behind, pulling her hair to one shoulder and the tip of my cock hitting her in the small of her back.

"Hands on the dresser, El Jefe," I whispered in her ear right before I bit her earlobe.

She complied, no questions asked, and I wondered what else I could ask her to do.

"Step your feet wide."

I waited until she did, then I ran my hand up her spine and pushed between her shoulder blades, lowering her upper body so her ass was in the air like a sweet invitation.

"Look at me."

Her eyes flew to meet my gaze in the mirror.

"Over there on the bed, you closed your eyes when you came. This time, you better be looking at me. Got it?"

Jesus, she was going to kill me. At the ripe old age of twenty-two I was going to have a heart attack from looking at the hottest woman who walked the planet. With each command I gave her, her eyes heated and her skin flushed hotter. She wanted me just as much as I wanted her.

I rolled on the condom and tilted her hips, notching the tip of my cock at her entrance and pushing all the way in with one thrust. She gasped, but didn't look away from my mirror image. My toes curled into the hotel carpet and I could have been done right then. But where was the fun in that?

So I pulled all the way out and reached down to massage up one of her legs, almost as happy to have my hand on any part of her skin. Then the other leg received the same attention. She pushed her hips even further back, squirming, wanting me to enter her again, but I wasn't going to give her what she wanted.

"My rule number one, El Jefe: you're not in control when the clothes are off. I am."

One eye twitched, but she didn't disagree.

I trailed one finger up the groove of her spine, reaching her hair. Using both hands, I pulled all her hair into my fist and gave it a tight tug. Her head tilted back and I slammed into her, a groan ripping from her throat.

One hand in her hair and the other on her hip, I set a punishing pace. Her eyes started to close. I tugged on her hair harder, arching her back. She gasped and her eyes flew open again, her hands straining to keep in contact with the dresser.

I clenched my jaw and tried to take in the vision of Elle in the mirror, her breasts swinging with each thrust into her hot, tight body. She'd completely submitted to me, something I never expected, hell, didn't even hope for.

I felt her legs trembling and had a moment of hesitation. Maybe I was being too rough with her. But then she was chanting my name and clenching around my dick. Her eyes stayed wide-open, her gaze never leaving me while she came undone. I was so focused on her, making sure I gave her every last second of pleasure I could, I didn't think about coming myself.

When she nearly collapsed onto the dresser, I pulled out and picked her up, carrying her to the bed. She opened her arms for me and I crawled in, both of us lying on our sides facing each other. Her limbs were limp and pliant. I pulled her leg over my hip and entered her slowly.

Her eyes fluttered open and I pressed my forehead to hers. Gently rocking, I found my release quickly, capturing her mouth and pouring everything I felt in that moment into the kiss.

Long minutes later, still inside her, she started talking, like I'd uncorked a well of conversation that only flowed when she was sated and well-fucked.

"You're so good, Austin."

"Why, thank you." I chuckled.

She slapped my chest half-heartedly. "No, silly man. I meant your cooking skills."

I kissed the top of her head. "Thanks, but I'm not sure what I'm even doing here. The other contestants have actual experience working in a kitchen and have even gone to school for it. I think I might only be here for comedic relief."

She lifted her head and the line between her eyebrows was back, the hazy eyes transforming with a fire that burned in its place. "Austin Cox, I don't ever want to hear you talk like that again. Do you really think I'd lie and say you're good when I don't think that? Really?"

I paused for a second, thinking it through. "No. You'd tell me how badly I sucked and then when I was crying, you'd tell me five more reasons why I sucked."

She thumped me on the chest. "Exactly! So start having some confidence about yourself."

I nodded slowly. "Okay, so dress better and have more confidence. Anything else I should be changing about myself?"

She gave me a look. "No, definitely not. The rest of you is magnificent."

"Wow. I've never been called magnificent before."

She pressed her lips to mine and settled back down in the crook of my arm. I lay still and lapped up the feeling of her in my arms. Her breath evened out and before long, she was asleep. And then so was I, a smile on my face all night.

"You can certainly expect some of the dishes to have a Spanish flair, but no, the restaurant will be largely North American steakhouse cuisine. I'm not striving to be the first restaurant of its kind. I want a place where every single dish is someone's favorite and the quality of food and service is excellent every single time you visit. A restaurant you can rely on for its excellence consistently."

My groggy eyes opened to Elle pacing the window of my hotel room, fully dressed in yesterday's clothes, minus the wedges. I had to blink a few times to come up to speed on all that had happened. She'd slept in my arms all night after making love to her several times, which had been a premature glimpse of heaven.

But waking up to her hard voice drilling into the phone while she was fully dressed was not how I would've planned our first morning together. With her back to me, I found my boxers and slid them on before getting up and making some coffee. When she heard me rummaging around, she turned around and gave me a grimace that was supposed to be a smile I'd bet. And a finger wave.

Yep, she let me fuck her brains out last night and now I only rated a finger wave.

I ran a hand through my hair and focused on making coffee. Maybe a caffeine injection would help me sort out what was going on here and what to do about it.

"Sure. You bet. I'll call you as soon as the menu is set. Okay. Thank you." Elle hung up and stayed facing the window for a moment.

I eyed her back, letting her take the lead. If she was pulling away from me, she'd need to say it out loud.

She hit some keys on her phone and then looked over her shoulder at me. "I have to make this call to my executive chef. Can you keep quiet?"

I nearly choked, letting out a sound that was half snort, half indignation. "I'll be as quiet as you were last night, El Jefe," I snapped, needing to remind her of how things had been, even if she wanted to pretend it never happened.

Her spine straightened and she didn't reply, simply hit a button and lifted the cell phone to her ear. I was dismissed.

Goddammit, she'd been so playful and open and warm last night, I was lulled into thinking she'd stay that way. That we'd broken through some barrier and were now steady on more intimate terms. Clearly, that was all wrong. I wasn't any closer than I'd been the day I walked in on her in her dressing room. The only difference was now I knew how she could be when she let down all her defenses.

I'd been intrigued with her before. Now I was haunted.

The coffee pot sputtered out two cups and I grabbed one, not even letting it cool. I needed caffeine, sooner rather than later. Elle started barking orders at her poor chef, something about a food critic wanting to write up the restaurant in an article about restaurants to watch.

The rolling desk chair was the perfect spot to sit and watch her work. Like a psychologist in his chair, trying to figure out the mind of the brilliant woman in front of him. I needed to figure out what switch got flipped in her head at some point between falling asleep and waking up this morning. Once I figured that out, I could make sure to stay far, far away from that toggle.

"I have to run to make it in time to the shoot today. Let's chat tonight and hammer out the details. Send me what you have in the meantime. Got it." She hung up and swung around finally, giving me her attention, but not her gaze.

"Gotta run," she said while slipping on her shoes and gathering her purse.

"How about a good-morning kiss first?" I ran a hand over my beard, giving her a chance to bridge the gap, but not expecting anything remotely warm.

She ignored me, walking to the door like I was nothing but a pack of those little donuts she loved so much: to be eaten when the craving struck, but hidden from the world as a shameful indulgence.

She got all the way to the door, her hand on the knob, when she spoke. "You're young. You don't understand responsibility. I have an entire staff and crew depending on me to get this restaurant open on time. I intend to make that happen."

A shot of pain raced through my body. She didn't know me at all. Responsibility? "Maybe you should get to know me before you start tossing out insults and judgements like that."

She didn't answer, just yanked the door open and left, her head held high, the wall rebuilt even higher.

The message was clear: she'd blocked me out.

Anger burned up my chest and I wished I were home. I'd call Marcos and meet him at the basketball court to beat the ever-loving shit out of my body, just to distract myself from the thoughts in my head.

I could understand Elle having dreams and wanting to make sure they came true. I was doing the same thing. Get a job as head chef in an upscale restaurant, get custody of my sister. The difference was, I'd never belittle her for her dream, or give mine more importance than hers. That was uncalled for.

My phone rang and I saw it was my sister calling. I packed away my anger and chatted with the woman in my life who actually meant everything. Time to screw my head on straight and get back to working on my own dream.

11

————

I was physically sick to my stomach. First, for having slept with a contestant on the show. Then for walking out on him in such a heartless way. *Dios mío*, he'd stood there all rumpled from sleep, his muscles popping everywhere, his hair gorgeously tousled from my hands gripping handfuls all night long. I'd wanted to strip naked again and pull his boxers down and show him how much I worshipped his body.

But the food critic was firing questions in my ear that had to be addressed. John was *the* food critic to get in your pocket if you wanted your restaurant to be a success. The construction of the inside of the space was moving forward while I was here in L.A., which meant I needed to be moving forward getting the menu set and organizing our suppliers. I'd neglected calling my executive chef the last few days because I'd been spending every moment either with Austin or thinking about Austin.

I needed to pull my head out this ridiculous non-relationship with a man far too young for me and remember my priorities. I was queasy, realizing I'd given him the wrong message by sleeping with him. And then I was hot and sweaty all over remembering him yanking on my hair and taking control of my body like some sort of Dom. I was no sub, but that had been blazing hot, like nothing I'd experienced before.

I headed to the offset location early, needing the help of makeup today. My trembling fingers were no match for winged eyeliner. I looked well rested, thanks to several orgasms that knocked me out right after. So there was always that.

By the time I was done in makeup, the cast and crew were all there, mingling around the park lawn, checking out the fire pits set up for the shoot. Tom called us all over and we had our morning meeting.

"No one is being voted off today, so enjoy that, but understand your performance here will be included in next challenge's decision." Tom was looking straight at Brandy and Austin.

I did a double take at Austin. His beard was gone, his fresh-faced chin completely free of scruff. I'd never seen him without at least a day or two of growth on his face. His black button-up shirt was tucked into charcoal gray dress pants and brown dress shoes. He looked like a professional.

He looked damn good.

I instantly missed "my" Austin with his ridiculous T-shirts and worn jeans.

"You'll have to start your own fire, make your own one-pot meal, and you've got one hour to do it. Make us proud, pioneers!" Tom took the bullhorn away from his mouth and the crew scattered to get ready for the shoot.

I joined Bertrand and Michael at the wooden picnic table we'd use as our judges' table for the day. Wardrobe had added a bit of flair by giving me a red plaid dress, albeit in a modern design. The gentlemen had matching red plaid handkerchiefs in the pockets of their suit jackets. Bertrand had even added a bolo tie I was quick to tease him about.

While the crew got the booms set up and checked lighting out here in the early morning sunshine, Austin and Brandy were chatting by their stations. Judging by the frowns and the heads in close proximity, it looked like a serious conversation. A frisson of fear started up in my stomach, mixing horribly with the nausea. I hoped our dirty laundry wasn't getting aired, to spread like wildfire amongst the cast and crew. I was fairly certain I could trust him not to say anything. Although I thought he'd understood my position a few days ago and then he was feeding me dessert with his own fingers in front of everyone.

The location manager was running around, making sure the area was blocked off appropriately so we didn't have extra extras in our shots of the challenge. Finally everything was set and Austin and Brandy broke apart to stand by their campfire stations. Tom quieted the set and we were filming.

"Welcome back to Taste Test, campfire edition!" Lindsey was full cowgirl in short shorts, boots, and a plaid shirt three sizes too small for her enlarged breasts. I supposed I should have counted myself lucky wardrobe hadn't had the same thing in mind for me.

Lindsey explained the rules and I tested out my own acting skills, smiling for the camera, making witty comments, and keeping my gaze away from the tall, handsome contestant who wouldn't leave my awareness. The challenge started and Austin and Brandy jumped into action.

I could finally look at him without him noticing, so I looked my fill, feasting on the sight of his body in that outfit, looking older than he ever had before. I knew exactly what he looked like out of the shirt and pants, how his skin jumped when I trailed my hand over him. How his abs flexed when he thrust...

I wrenched my thoughts away from last night with difficulty. Instead, I focused on Lindsey and the way she was paying all kinds of attention to Austin today. My money was on her noticing his outfit and wanting to see where some flirting could lead. Austin laughed and smiled like normal as he got his fire going quickly and went to work on his meal. He looked perfectly at ease, which irritated me as much as him talking quietly with Brandy had earlier.

Was he unaffected by last night? Did he write me off as a crazy lady? Or maybe I was some sort of conquest. See if he could land the judge. Well done, Austin. Your hugs and your laugh worked like a charm.

No, no, that wasn't right either. He wanted more this morning. I was the one to run, not him. I just needed him to understand that being with him couldn't take away from my priorities. If he could deal with that, then maybe we could work something out.

"So, we should be done here shortly. Wanna grab dinner after the taping?" Michael bumped me suggestively with his elbow. I'd forgotten he was even a part of this show. He'd left me alone since the first day. I'd hoped he got the message that I wasn't interested.

"You do know our mics are on, right?" I looked back at the contestants, hoping he'd move away. No such luck.

"Who cares? Some guy lucky to even have a job is hearing me ask you out. So, dinner tonight?"

Trying to hold in the grimace, I replied, "No, thanks, I'm good."

Michael walked in front of me, blocking my view of Austin and Brandy. "Oh, come on. We're stuck here for a little longer. Might as well blow off some steam. Hell, us going out might stir up some publicity for the show. Tom'd love it."

I rolled my eyes. "I don't give a shit if Tom would love it. *I* don't love it. I already said no politely, so here's my not-so-polite version: hell no."

I stepped around him, but he followed me. Where was Bertrand when you needed him?

"Really? You're going to turn me down but sleep with the contestant? I'm pretty sure that won't go over well with Tom."

My heart stopped and fear crawled up my spine. I spun around and walked back to him, my voice hushed. "What did you say?"

He leaned in closer, his rancid breath hitting my face. "You heard me. Going for the real young ones, huh?"

I wanted to wipe the smile off his face. With my nails. Remembering the microphones pinned to our outfits, I had to shut him down before the whole crew knew. Quickly. "I don't know what you're talking about." I looked down at the mic on the neckline of my dress and then lifted my eyebrow at Michael.

His grin grew and then he winked at me. "Must have misunderstood. We can talk about it tonight at dinner."

"Right after the show. Hotel restaurant." I walked away, head held high, even though I wanted to fling myself to the ground and cry. This was exactly why I shouldn't have gotten involved with Austin. I should have known better.

I got through the rest of the show, my smile frozen, my cheeks aching with the effort to hold that grin in place. Both dishes by the contestants were delicious even if my abused stomach would only allow me a bite or two. I thought Austin's chili was better than Brandy's stew, but then again, I wasn't exactly neutral anymore, was I? Yet another reason I should have walked away from Austin and the magic of his orgasms.

As soon as Tom yelled "cut," I ripped the microphone off my dress and gathered my things.

"Meet you there," Michael said loudly before walking to his car.

I didn't exactly know how to handle this situation. Did Michael actually see us going to Austin's room last night, or was he bluffing? Maybe he saw the way Austin and I looked at each other and assumed? Either way, I was denying everything. We'd have dinner, I'd make it clear there was nothing to blackmail me over, and I'd go to my room. Alone.

Brandy was parked next to my car, struggling to get all her

utensils into the back of her car. I looked around for a member of the crew, or even Austin, but no one was around.

"Here. Let me help you." I grabbed a box that was slipping off the top of the stack in her arms and got it into her trunk.

"Oh, thank you! Didn't seem like that much until I got halfway across the parking lot. It's like a twenty-acre lot." She giggled and I couldn't help but smile.

"You did great today. You ready for the final round?" I ran my hands over the strap of my handbag, feeling awkward, like I'd chosen sides in some little game she had no awareness of.

She grinned easily, not weighed down by guilt, fear, and disappointment, the trio of best friends that followed me everywhere today. "I sure hope so! This whole thing has been so exciting. I still can't believe I'm even here. I mean, I want to win this thing, but now that I know Austin's story, I'll be happy if he wins too, you know?"

I tilted my head. "What do you mean?"

"Well, he has such a beautiful reason for being here. To be able to adopt his little sister? That would be amazing. Heck, if I win, I might even feel a little guilty. Poor guy, that was a rough break."

The wind started blowing and my hair danced around my face. The rest of the world faded into the background as I stared at Brandy. She was still talking, but I couldn't hear what she was saying. All I could hear were her words echoing through my head, "adopt his little sister." What did that mean? Why didn't I know this about him?

Why hadn't I asked?

I turned abruptly and hopped in my car. I didn't even know if Brandy was still talking. All I knew was I had to be alone. I needed to think. I needed to sort through everything that had happened the last few days with this new information. I'd thrown Austin's age in his face and told him he didn't understand responsibility. If I hadn't left his room this morning, he would have had every right to throw me out.

¿Qué hice?

As I pulled up to the hotel, I saw Michael waiting outside the lobby doors, probably worried I'd blow him off and not show up for this ridiculous dinner. I gave myself two full breaths before I smoothed my hair back and climbed out of the car. I needed him to be quiet. Would it take a favor to buy his silence? Or something even worse?

~

The snake had the *cojones* to put his hand on my lower back as we walked through the restaurant to our table. I allowed it, even as it made my skin crawl. Placing my purse on the chair with me, I sat across from him, my back straight and my icy glare carrying my message for me: don't fuck with me.

"Don't look so scary, Elle. It's just you and me. Let's talk." Michael had the nerve to smile while he attempted to blackmail me, looking like the lecher my instincts warned me about on day one.

"Yes, let's talk so this ridiculous dinner can be over that much sooner." I smiled, the cat about to eat the mouse, right after charming it into thinking it was safe. "Again, Michael, I don't know what you think you saw, but there's no meat to your claim. I truly don't enjoy being falsely accused of things of this nature. I would take that into consideration next time you decide to threaten me."

His sneer stayed in place, though it wobbled a bit on the edges. "Oh, this isn't a threat, Elle. I saw you walk into Austin's room yesterday and you didn't come out. Floor five, remember?"

Nausea flared to life in my stomach at his accurate information, but I scoffed, playing the part, no matter what it took. "Michael. I went to his room to sign his cookbook. Did you know he has my cookbook? It's quite flattering really. But I left right after. You must have missed my departure."

"I highly doubt that, but it doesn't really matter, does it? A rumor like that doesn't need proof before it spreads like a bad virus, affecting everyone. So, what's it worth to you, Elle?"

I gritted my teeth and narrowed my eyes, thoroughly disgusted by the man in front of me. "So, that's it? You're going to blackmail me without proof? For what? What do you want, Michael Fin?"

He settled back in his chair, confident he had me right where he wanted me. "I want a job as the head chef at your new restaurant. Relocating to the East Coast is looking enticing and your restaurant would be ideal. You and I could be a force. Together."

I sneered. What a dirtbag. "What happened to your restaurant in Beverly Hills?"

He shrugged. "Creative differences with the owner."

Yeah, I'd bet. More like fired for being the worthless sack he was. It was time to end this debacle. "I'm afraid I already hired an executive chef, so I'm fresh out of positions. Good luck to you." I went to grab my purse, but he leapt across the table to grab my arm, stopping me.

"I don't think you get it. Give me this position or I'll go to the press." His teeth were bared, that vein in his forehead more pronounced as he spat the words at me.

"Take your hand off me now." I glared right back, feeling safe since we were in a public space, though my heart raced. I wouldn't show the fear that shot through my body, wouldn't give him that satisfaction. When he released my arm and sat back down, smoothing his tie, I pulled out my cell phone.

"Next time you try to blackmail someone, make sure they aren't recording the whole thing." I wiggled my phone in the air, a smug grin in full force.

His eyes went wide before his whole face turned a dark shade of red. "You're bluffing." His voice was low, tilting up at the end, the question mark implied, whether he meant to or not.

"Unlike you, I get solid evidence before threatening someone. You better hope a rumor doesn't start about me or I'll assume it was you and this recording gets leaked. Your career, such as it is, will be over. *¿Comprende?*"

I jumped up and threw my phone back in my purse before sweeping out of the restaurant with all the dignity I could muster. I held it together until the elevator doors closed and then I slumped against the back wall. My hands were shaking and I could barely take a deep breath. Somehow, I made it into my room.

I sat down on the bed and put my head in my hands. How had I gotten here? Everything was such a mess and I had myself to blame for all of it. I should have never slept with Austin. He was ten years younger than me and a contestant on this show. My whole reason for being here was to generate good press for my restaurant opening, not to start an affair with a cast member. And then I hurt Austin in the process by throwing false accusations and hope at him. Now this.

Because contrary to what I told Michael, I hadn't recorded a thing. I didn't have concrete proof any more than he did. All I had was a tiny thread of hope to hang onto that he would believe me and not start a rumor.

My entire career depended on it.

ustin

Yesterday was a clusterfuck. I was so pissed when Elle left my room, I'd shaved my beard off Britney Spears style in a fit of rage and got all dressed up, my only focus on proving her wrong.

She was all kinds of wrong. Responsibility was an old friend of mine. Elle's arrival had merely made me put it on the back burner, but no more.

Then I got to the location and I had to pretend there was nothing going on between Elle and me, which was so stupid. I could have started that damn fire pit solely with the electricity that seemed to arc between her and me with just one look. It took every ounce of willpower I had in my body to keep from reminiscing on every moment we'd shared the night before. I was angry and horny at the same time. Hongry.

The conversation with Brandy before the challenge had been a nice distraction. I was realizing I was lonely being here all by myself without someone to confide in. I couldn't tell her about what was forefront on my mind—damn Elle and her ability to distract me from what mattered most—but at least I got to tell her about my sister. And she told me about her family, her dreams, her plans for after the show.

Brandy's well-thought-out plans got me thinking about mine. I needed to sit down with Bertrand and Michael before the show was over and see if I could get an introduction to a chef in the Northern California area. I'd need a job the minute I left L.A. if I was to get established and get my sister back. No matter what had happened, I was starting to get more confidence in my skills, thanks to Elle. For that at least, I'd always be grateful.

Today was a day off, so I slept in and then took a shower. When I stepped out of the bathroom, towel around my hips, I intended to order room service as I was starving, but my phone pinged several times. I picked it up, shocked to see Elle reaching out.

Elle: *I'm sure you want nothing to do with me, but we need to talk.*
Elle: *Can you meet me in my room? I don't want anyone seeing.*
Elle: *Please?*

Fuck. It was the "please" that got me. I didn't know what she wanted to talk about, but the side of me that still went weak in the knees when I thought about those lips couldn't say no.

"Great, come to L.A. and I turn into some kind of masochist. Just fuckin' great," I muttered as I whipped my towel off and found some clean boxers. Next was jeans and my favorite T-shirt —The Handsome & the Beast Saloon. She wouldn't get my fancy shirts, and I hoped the name of the bar on my shirt would resonate with her. Hopefully she'd know which character she was.

I was still angry, but more than that, I was hurt. She'd made it look so easy to turn off her emotions and push me out. She didn't want anyone to see us talking? Fucking hell, that really made a guy feel real good. I made up my mind: I'd be her dirty little secret one more time so she could say whatever she had to say and then I'd take my toys and go home.

Austin: *I've only got a few minutes so you'll have to make it quick. What's your room number?*

Elle: *Thank you. Room 718.*

I knocked on her door, looking up and down her hallway while I waited, wondering what the hell I was doing there. I guess I needed to be lashed by her sharp tongue one last time.

She swung the door open and my heart instantly dropped. She looked terrible and perfect, all at the same time. She didn't have any makeup on, her hair was a curly mess down her back, and she was in a long, well-worn T-shirt. I was still a hot-blooded male, so my mind instantly went to the question as to whether she had anything on under that shirt. She may be a bitch at times, but she was a damn gorgeous one.

She waved me in and then retreated to the window, where she paced, the curtains still drawn. The door closed behind me and it got dark in the room. I couldn't see much, but I could smell bacon. And maybe pancakes.

"You wanna turn a light on so I can see you? Or is this your secret den where you kill young men after you've lured them in with breakfast?"

Her head whipped up and a ghost of a smile crossed her features. "I don't know what to do. I need your help."

Fuck me sideways if that cry for help didn't puff up my chest and make me want to swoop in like a knight in shining armor.

"What's the problem?" I stayed where I was, barely inside her room, still not wanting to come too close even though I wanted to race over and hold her, never to let go.

She laughed, not her usual pretty kind. The kind that grates and doesn't exude happiness. "Michael saw me go into your room the other day." My heart stuttered to a stop. "He tried to blackmail himself into a job at my new restaurant last night. I lied and said I recorded our whole conversation. I don't know if he believed me or not. I've been all over the web this morning, but there's been no ties mentioned between you and me. Not yet."

I grabbed a handful of hair, the implications of it all filtering through my mind. "Damn. I'm sorry, Elle. I know what's in jeopardy here. What can I do?"

She threw her hands in the air. "Not much either of us can do, right? I mean, we slept together. Can't put the horse back in the barn."

I scrunched up my face. "Am I the horse in this scenario or are you referring to my cock?"

"Austin! Be serious." She looked ready to murder me. Though seeing a little fire back in her eyes was a good thing.

I held my hands out in surrender. "I'm sorry! I like to use jokes to diffuse tension. So sue me."

She put her hands on her hips. "It gets worse. My mother called again last night and is trying to force her new boyfriend on me. He's a brand-new chef and Mother thinks he should be my executive chef, even though he has zero experience. She even went behind my back and called my actual chef to harass him and try to get him to work with her boyfriend. Never mind this is my business, not hers. Now my chef is threatening to quit because he doesn't want to be in the middle of family drama."

She was pacing faster, her hands lashing out at the air like it'd personally offended her. And like the immature asshole I was, I kept glancing down at the hem of her T-shirt. Every time she slashed the air, the hem rode higher and I got just a little bit closer to answering the question of panties or no panties.

But then she was right in front of me, her finger jabbing me in the chest. "And then there's you!"

"Whoa, what about me?" I didn't really want to be the center of her attention at the moment, not with steam coming out her ears and her eyes flashing bright with irritation.

"Everything's about you, Austin!" She started counting off on her fingers, unaware her accent was getting thicker and thicker.

Much like my cock. "You drive me crazy with all your smiles and laughing and jokes. Like, who's seriously that happy all the time? You drive me crazy in bed. And I shouldn't want more, but I do. You don't tell me anything real about yourself and then I find out these things from Brandy and feel guilty for being a *puta*. And you don't get out of my head!"

Her hands went back to her hips, the movement straining the T-shirt across her chest, which gave me full access to the outline of her nipples. Well, there was one answer: no bra. My brain finally kicked into gear and I realized what she said. Hot damn, the woman still wanted me. Then why did I still feel like shit?

I scrubbed the heels of my hands over my eyes. "Wait. Hold on a second. Let's go through this, huh? Yes, I am a happy guy and I like to joke around. You should try it more often. Kind of like practicing hugging. Second, you drive me just as wild in bed and I'll always want more. I would have told you all about myself, but the minute you were done with me, you jumped out of bed and ran away. That's on you, not me." I reached out and put my hands on her hips, right below her fists. "And I'm in your head because you like me. Admit it." I smirked at her, knowing it would piss her off.

Flames danced in her eyes before they melted in front of me, going hazy as she looked her fill. Her finger came up and traced the dimples on each side of my smile. "I hate that I've never seen these dimples. Don't ever have a beard again," she whispered.

"What is that, rule number eight?" I whispered back, pulling her in closer.

"Fuck the rules." Her arms snaked around my neck and I dipped my head to press my lips to hers. Her tongue swooped in like she couldn't get close enough and I followed suit, needing more of this woman. I was still holding onto a kernel of anger toward her, but I couldn't deny that I still wanted her. I didn't want to be her dirty little secret, and I was more than a little afraid she'd treat me like a stranger again tomorrow, but it wasn't enough to keep me from her now.

I pulled back and swiped my thumb across the dusting of white sugar on the side of her mouth. "I see you had your nasty donuts, but did you order me breakfast?"

She quickly wiped her face and tried to duck her head. Then she straightened up and licked my dimple, nodding. "Are you telling me you need to eat first?"

I contemplated what I was most hungry for. "Why don't I eat while we get naked? I'm an excellent multitasker."

Her brow furrowed and I laughed. She had no idea what fun I could have with some good old-fashioned maple syrup. I finally got my answer—panties—when I lifted up her shirt and drew it over her head.

"Fuck, Elle, you're so beautiful," I whispered. I told my stomach to shut up so I could devour her, but he let out a pathetic growl that filled the room. Elle laughed, the sound beautiful and carefree, so I forgave my stomach for its ill-timed protest.

"Lie on the bed and get those panties off, woman," I practically growled at her.

Her eyes heated and she instantly obeyed. I was hard enough to pound out a chicken breast. However, I didn't think our producer would find that tool to meet the sanitary standards for the show.

Never taking my eyes off her sprawled on the bed and ready for me, I lifted the silver lid from the plate sitting on the desk. I grabbed a pancake and the little white ceramic pot of syrup and headed her way. I crawled up her body on my knees, holding the pot in the air above her breasts.

"Austin..." she warned.

I tipped the pot ever so slightly, a drizzle of syrup landing on her nipple and cascading down the side of her breast. Elle gasped at the contact. I quickly righted the pot and leaned down to lick up the sticky mess and took a bite of the pancake in my left hand.

"Delicious," I murmured. She was breathing faster and looked hungry too, so I fed her a bite of the pancake. "Syrup?" She nodded.

I climbed up higher and drizzled some onto my cock, like hot fudge on a banana split. Her eyes went molten right before she opened her mouth and wrapped those lips around my cock. Her tongue peeked out and swirled around the tip before she took me all the way in, her neck straining to lift her head off the bed. I nearly dumped the rest of the syrup in her hair when my muscles gave out on me.

Thankfully for her, I was able to set the damn thing down on the bedside table, along with the crumpled pancake before extricating myself.

"Jesus, woman." I uttered the words on a shiver, needing to slow things down or I wouldn't last. She giggled—actually giggled—and then pouted.

"Hey, I wasn't done with my sausage."

"You'll get plenty of sausage later. Right now, I need that bacon." I lifted off her and grabbed several pieces from the food tray. I ate some as I walked back, then broke off a piece for her, feeding it to her slowly. When I'd fed her that apple pie bite on camera, everyone had been watching and I'd had to keep it PG. Now I could slow down and watch her like I wanted, nibbling on that pouty lower lip any time I desired.

When we finished it all, she licked my fingers clean, pulling my thumb into her mouth to suck and lave it with her tongue. Then she popped it out with a smile. "Sure I can't get some of that sausage now?"

"Nope. I've still got two pancakes over there to finish."

I grabbed the food, along with a towel from her bathroom. I threw the towel at her and she spread it out beneath her.

"So conscientious," she teased me.

I lifted a shoulder. "I'm pretty responsible."

That dig hit the bull's-eye. Her cheeks flushed and she looked down. "I'm sorry," she whispered.

"I know." As much as I loved hearing an apology, I was also sorry I'd brought it up and killed the playful mood. "Ready to get sticky?"

This time, I rolled the pancakes like a burrito and took a huge bite before setting them down again. The syrup pot was still mostly full and I intended to ingest every last drop before I was done. I started drizzling up her thighs, her squirms and squeals egging me on. Setting the pot aside, I got to work moving her legs apart and licking up her thighs. When I reached the juncture of her legs, her whole body shuddered with just a fan of my breath.

What a dilemma. I had half a pot of syrup left.

I reached for it again and abandoned my position, smiling like a loon when I heard her loud groan of protest. "I'm just so hungry…" I teased. The rest of my pancakes went in my mouth and I hurried to chew and swallow. This was fun teasing her, but it was also delaying my own satisfaction and I couldn't take much more of it.

The pot tipped for the last time, emptying all the syrup onto her breasts and sliding down her sides in an epic mess. She yelped and nearly came off the bed had I not been straddling her hips. I lapped up all I could, but alas, the mess was too big for one tongue.

"Dammit, Austin!" She bucked, her hips jabbing me forward, my knees shuffling to keep upright. Right into the pools of syrup on each side of her. Then her mouth closed around my cock and my eyes rolled back in my head. Nothing mattered except for the warm cave my cock was now living in.

"Fuckkkkk…" My sticky hands rested on the headboard, holding on for dear life while she attacked me from below. A loud whack reverberated through the room and then my ass cheek lit up like a Christmas tree.

She'd spanked me.

"Rule number one, El Jefe." I reminded her through my teeth. We were both struggling to have the upper hand here. She had my most delicate body part in her mouth, right by her teeth. But spanking me? That was pushing it.

I reached back and found her legs spread where I'd left them. I dipped and thrust a finger at an angle and hit pay dirt. Her mouth opened on a moan and I took the opportunity to slip free of her and hop off the bed. A loud "schloop" noise echoed in the room, like boots trying to step free of a huge mud puddle. It was actually my knees unsticking from the big stain of syrup on the bath towel.

I reached down to help her up, but the bath towel stayed affixed to her back like we'd used glue, not syrup. She looked ridiculous standing there with a towel as her shadow.

Elle started giggling and I couldn't help but join in. What the hell was going on here? I mean, we were chefs. Meaning we were the most qualified to be handling food and know what to do with it. Food fights were supposed to be sexy, weren't they? I put a hand on my knee to support myself while I belly laughed.

Elle wiped tears from her face, still laughing. "Shower?"

I couldn't even answer, but headed in that direction with her, the towel trailing her the entire way. After getting the water nice and warm, I picked her up under the arms and placed her in while trying to pry the towel off her back. When the last of the devil sauce, known as maple syrup, went down the drain and the laughter dried up, I picked her up and her legs went around my waist.

"I've been working on my hugs," she whispered in my ear, her arms around my neck.

I placed her gently against the tile wall and slid into her. "You're turning into the best hugger I've ever met." My forehead lowered to hers and with eyes on each other, sharing breath, sharing ourselves, I spilled myself into her. And she welcomed me.

13
___

I spent another few hours in the makeup chair, having the professionals do their magic since today was the last day of shooting, if all went well. A stunning dark red dress was waiting for me in my dressing room with tall black stilettos to hobble my feet all day. I couldn't believe the end of filming was already here. Given that Taste Test was a pilot, there were only five episodes to gauge the audience's reaction. If it went over well, further seasons would be scheduled and filmed, which might or might not include an invite for me to come back as a judge.

The whole two hours in makeup were spent thinking about Austin and how last night was so different than anything I'd experienced before. I'd never made love to a man with comfortable laughter and the level of intensity that I did with Austin. He'd accepted my apology, though I could tell he was still hurt by my actions. The whole time we were exploring each other's body, there was an undercurrent of hesitation. Of worry.

I was worried about Michael and my reputation. He was probably worried I'd turn on him again and I'm sure he had his sister on his mind.

However, the only truly bad part of the night had been when Austin had to leave at three in the morning to sneak back to his room. That part felt dirty. It also reminded me of Michael and his threats. There wasn't anything else I could do but hope he kept his mouth shut. I didn't like control of the situation not being within my grasp.

So there I sat squirming for two hours, alternatively turned on thinking about Austin and the things he did to me in the shower, and then sick to my stomach that everything was going to blow up somehow.

"Ten minutes!" a crew member yelled into the room. Bertrand looked stressed as he and the hairdresser fussed with his hairs. I think the poor guy had lost another one since filming began. At this point, he'd do better to just shave it bald and work the tough-guy angle. I wasn't going to be the one to tell him, though. I needed at least one friend on the judges' panel.

With only a few minutes to spare, I ran into my dressing room and got in the dress and heels. Hell, I'd need all three minutes left to carefully step my way out to the set in those damn things.

Right as I reached the edge of the set, in front of the rings of cameras, my heel slid and I wobbled, about to go down. A steady hand appeared to grab my elbow and yank me up. I'd know that hand anywhere. That hand had been all over my body last night.

I flushed immediately and willed the blood to go somewhere else. I couldn't be standing here blushing with Michael in the shadows watching. Pulling my arm free, I decided to do what Austin was always advising me to do.

I showed off jazz hands and then pointed at my feet. "Just learned how to walk. Thanks for the assist." I grinned at Austin, overly cheerful to mask how uncomfortable I truly was.

He gave me an equally awkward smile back and a thumbs-up

before moving to his station next to Brandy. They hugged it out while I slowly made my way to the judges' table, being more careful not to fall in front of everyone. Snails could literally have beat me to my chair.

"Goodness, sit down before you hurt yourself, Elle. Those shoes are to die for, but they must be hell to walk in." Bertrand hopped up and took me by the elbow, making sure I got to my seat safely.

Once there, the sound guys came around to get our microphones set up. Michael was boring holes into the side of my head the entire time. I kept my RBF in full effect, hoping he wouldn't risk provoking me. And I certainly didn't look in Austin's direction. I was on stage here just as much as the contestants were and I couldn't screw up now. Being seen walking into Austin's hotel room was bad enough. Any slip-up now and Michael would pounce. I could feel it.

"Welcome back to the last episode of Taste Test where we see who our big winner will be!" Lindsey started the show, being her usual cheerleader self. She interviewed each of us, getting soundbites post production would use to jack up the drama and hook viewers. As much as her constant hip-hip-hurray attitude irritated me, she was good at her job and I could see why Tom hired her for the position. In an odd way, I'd miss her just as much as everyone else when the show was over. Well, everyone except for Austin.

My brain was having a hard timing coming to terms that win or lose, today was the last day I'd be around Austin. We hadn't talked about it last night, but it was there in the background, casting shadows over a perfect evening. He never brought up trying to see me after the show was over and I couldn't seem to get the words out of my tight throat either.

"Welcome back to Taste Test, where we put our contestants to the test with random challenges and mean judges." Lindsey gave the judges' panel a mean face and we laughed right on cue.

"Today's challenge is simple: cook an entree worthy of stardom while using one mandatory ingredient..." She paused for maximum effect. "Squid."

Dios mío, not at all what my stomach needed today. Squid had to be cooked just right to make it the proper texture. A second too long and it was rubbery. A second not long enough and you made your taste tester sick. The crew brought out displays of squid meant to gross out the television audience, which I could attest was very effective.

"You'll have exactly two hours to prepare your dish. Are you ready, contestants?" Lindsey looked at Austin and Brandy, who nodded their agreement. I flickered my gaze over Austin. The sight made my stomach drop even further. He looked gorgeous in fitted black slacks and a deep blue polo.

But he wasn't smiling.

Something wasn't right, but I didn't know what. Was it the thought of trying to cook squid? The thought of saying goodbye to each other? Or was he regretting last night? Either way, there wasn't time to ask him as Lindsey started the challenge and he and Brandy jumped into action.

While they cooked, the cameras got more interviews with each judge, wanting us to highlight the difficulties with cooking squid. Then Lindsey went around to both stations getting shots of what they were in the middle of preparing, probably making them even more nervous.

Bertrand and I kept up easy conversation while Michael was oddly quiet. He usually joked around or at least tried to be friendly. Today you could practically feel the waves of hostility coming off of him. Even Bertrand looked at me with raised eyebrows. I shrugged, acting like I had no idea what was going on with him.

Finally Lindsey called time and the contestants stepped away from their dishes. The crew cleared the plates and brought them in front of us, Brandy's first. She'd made a pasta dish with homemade red sauce and deep fried, breaded squid on top. It presented well and first bite in, I could tell she had a winner. The squid was cooked just right and the taste blended well with the tomato sauce and pasta. The other judges agreed with me.

Next up was Austin's dish: a squid risotto with tomato, brandy, and cream sauce. It was remarkably good, the sauce being to-die-for, but the squid was just okay for me. I said as much, saying I liked a crunchy fried squid to hide what I was actually eating, which got a few laughs and was also the truth, but I could see Austin's face fall. My ribs squeezed around my chest. I didn't want to hurt him, but it was my duty as a judge to be honest with my assessment. Whether we slept together or not, that's how I would have called it.

Michael perked up beside me and roasted Austin next. His harsh opinion was quite shocking. Even Lindsey was at a loss for words. Anger burned through the guilt in my chest with each nasty thing he said. He was doing it simply to attack Austin for personal reasons, which was beyond unfair.

Bertrand was thankfully last, with absolutely glowing things to say about Austin's dish, even going so far as to say it was his favorite from the whole show. My heart was ready to beat right out of my chest. This was the moment. I could already see how this would go down. Bertrand would vote for Austin, Michael would vote for Brandy. And I would be left to place the deciding vote.

Me.

The judge who was sleeping with one of the contestants.

You know those moments in life where all your doubts and vulnerabilities crystallize into one moment of startling clarity? That was my moment right there. When everything I'd been worried about narrowed down into one thought: what the fuck have you done, Elle?

I was so close to realizing my dream of opening my own

restaurant. I just had to get through the taping of this short reality show and then it would be mine. That's all I had to do.

But no. I'd let myself get swept away by a twenty-two-year-old man-boy who gave good hugs and had dimples I wanted to move into and set up house. I'd let him talk me into having *feelings* and *smiling*. This is exactly why I shied away from attachments and taking days off. Because the minute you relaxed and had a few out-of-this-world orgasms you were staring into a bright light and being asked to make a decision that would affect everything in your future.

So I made the only choice that would put things back on the right track. The only choice I knew how to make. It was time to step up and be El Jefe.

"Elle Fierro. Looks like you have the deciding vote! Who's going to be our big winner of the Taste Test?" Lindsey was smiling like she had no idea about the gravity of this decision, because she truly didn't. No one did. Except Austin.

With Michael's gaze burning one side of my face and Austin's desperate gaze on the other, I opened my mouth one last time.

"Brandy Latrell."

Confetti burst from the rafters and everyone clapped. Lindsey jumped up and down and handed flowers to Brandy. Michael and Bertrand stood, clapping for our winner.

Austin and I were the only two people on the whole set frozen, oblivious to the celebration around them. My gaze finally settled on him, my conscience needing to see the devastation on his face.

My penance was his expression, forever in my memory, burned there to taunt me at night when I was alone. Too late, I realized what he meant to me. How much I believed in him. How much I wanted to see him succeed. But I'd spoken and now I'd ripped his dream away from him so I could realize mine.

"Glad you came to your senses," Michael whispered in my ear, his hand on my shoulder. I shrugged his hand off, but still he spoke. "Guess I was wrong about you after all. I'm sure we can still be friends."

If he was waiting for an answer, my only response was a lethal glare. Suddenly, I couldn't stay here one second longer. I leaned down and took off my ridiculous shoes. Then I stepped off the platform and walked off the set.

To hell with this show. To hell with Michael. To hell with my imploding career.

The last thing I heard was Lindsey interviewing Austin and his voice coming out strained, like a band was pulling tighter and tighter across his throat. "I did my best, but sometimes you gotta admit defeat."

Whether he was speaking about the show or our relationship, I'd never be sure.

I needed to escape somewhere private and lick my wounds. Figure out where I was going to go from here. Here being this "rock bottom" everyone talked about, but I'd never experienced. The place where all dreams are either smashed to smithereens or dulled to something so faded, you can't remember why you wanted it in the first place.

Because now that I'd destroyed Austin's dreams, I couldn't seem to care about my own. Ironic, huh?

I'd almost made it to my dressing room when Bertrand's voice echoed down the hallway. "Elle, wait!" I heard his footsteps approaching at a fast pace, and for the life of me, I couldn't ditch him. The guy shouldn't be running at his age and I wasn't going to be the reason he had a heart attack.

I stopped in my tracks and waited for him to join me. When his panting breaths were right beside me, I looked over, waiting for him to speak.

He caught sight of my face and his eyes widened. "What's wrong, darling?"

Only then did I realize I had tears racing down my cheeks. I couldn't remember the last time I cried, let alone cried in public. I wiped away all traces as quickly as I could and grabbed Bertrand in a hug. He was frail and smelled like Old Spice. He seemed shocked I'd hug him, but he recovered quickly and put his arms around my waist for a quick squeeze. Even Bertrand knew how to hug without being taught.

"Thank you for being my friend, Bertrand. Goodbye," I whispered in his ear. I released him and ran the rest of the way to my room, not stopping until my door was locked shut behind me.

I sat in a chair, my legs curled up under me, not even bothering to turn on the light in my dressing room. The darkness was what I wanted. I wanted to completely melt into it and disappear. I wallowed in my pity for several hours, until I knew all cast and crew had left the studio. Until I knew I could escape without being seen.

I emerged from that dressing room a new woman.

This was my life now. I was on my way to realizing my every dream.

Who cared that all the color was gone around me, leaving only shades of gray, acquaintances who never hugged, and easy laughter that never filled my ears?

Not me.

I was El Jefe.

14

ustin

On the pisstivity scale, I was off the charts. Simple expressions like mad as hell, fit to be tied, angry like a crack whore late to pick up her kid stuck in traffic on the 405...none of them held a candle to what I was feeling.

Either that or I cooked some bad squid.

My stomach was knotted like a pretzel and I couldn't decide if I wanted to laugh or cry. So I smiled. And I joked. And I congratulated Brandy like the goddamn adult I was. Some of us couldn't run off the set and hide like a coward.

And when I'd done my duty, I wiped the smile from my face and drove back to the hotel in a perpetual red haze. I didn't like losing. No one did.

But I especially didn't like losing because the woman I'd slept with sold me out to some sleazeball. I saw Michael staring her down at the taping today and I saw her squirming in her chair.

She voted against me to get Michael off her back so she could ensure her restaurant would thrive.

She crushed my dream so she could have hers.

Plain and simple. Now I'd have to look into my sister's pleading eyes and tell her I didn't win, I didn't have a job, and I'd have to make her wait even longer before I could get her out of whatever foster home she'd been shuffled to this week.

So you see, Elle hadn't just crushed my dream, she'd crushed my life. I wasn't on this show for fame and fortune or to prove my mommy wrong in some twisted psychologist's wet dream like she was. I was simply in it to get my sister back.

By the time I reached my room and started throwing clothes into my duffle bag with far more energy than was necessary for packing a few T-shirts, I reached another conclusion: I only had myself to blame.

And wasn't that a pisser of a conclusion?

I was the one who let my desire for her take over my common sense. She'd warned me away left and right, in English and in Spanish. She essentially walked around with a giant stop sign on her forehead with the perennial straight face and rigid posture. I was the dumbass who disregarded all the red flags and pushed her to be someone she wasn't. Her real nature had won out in the end when she threw me under the bus without a flutter of an eyelash.

And *that* Elle? That wasn't a woman I wanted anything to do with. As much as it felt like a funhouse illusion, it sure seemed like that cold-hearted version *was* the real Elle, whether my pansy-ass heart wanted to believe it or not.

When my flight landed in Sacramento the following morning, I felt like I was landing on the moon. Everything looked different, felt different. I'd gone to war and lost, both the show and the woman. I felt like I'd aged a year for every day I was gone, the experience in L.A. bringing a maturity I wasn't looking for, but got anyway.

I was back home, but my heart wasn't in it. I wasn't sure where the hell my heart was, but it wasn't with Elle and it wasn't here. Maybe it was in a meat grinder somewhere. Which would explain the extreme pain and inability to take a deep breath.

But Austin Cox wasn't a quitter.

When the going got tough, I threw on my favorite T-shirt—or whichever one was clean—and gave myself the mother of all pep talks, which usually involved talking about myself in the third person.

Totally normal, nothing to see here.

By the time the Uber driver dropped me off in front of the apartment I shared with Marcos, I was hopped up on artificial confidence and overstated belief in myself. Which meant it was the perfect time to call my sister and make sure she knew I was one step closer to taking care of her. She didn't need to know that the one step hadn't actually happened yet, but I had a plan. A solid one.

"Austin? Did you win??" Abi's voice squealed into the phone so loud I had to pull it away from my ear the minute she answered.

A stab of pain hit me in the gut at her enthusiasm and trust. I threw my duffle bag on my bed and paced the tiny, empty apartment.

"Well, not quite, Abilene." Step number one of evading little sister's questions was to irritate her with the use of her full name. "I came in second place, but lost the big challenge at the end. The damn squid got me."

"Huh? So, what does that mean? Second place, not the squid. Ew." I could practically hear her nose scrunching up from over the phone line. She'd once cried over a shrimp dinner, so overcome with emotion for the poor shellfish she couldn't eat it. Squid was in the same category as shrimp I imagined.

I ran a hand over my hair and pulled on all my years of spinning the positive in each shitty situation life presented. "Means I made a ton of contacts with professional chefs who loved my skills. Gotta make a few phone calls and get a job set up and then I'm coming for you."

She squealed again. "You gonna wear that big white chef's hat?"

I chuckled. "Yeah, the tallest, biggest one I can find. Just for you."

"I miss you, Austin."

"Miss you too, Abi. I'll call you as soon as I have a job lined up, okay?"

"Go get 'em, tiger!"

My sister. Always my biggest cheerleader.

That hit me square in the feels and I decided I was allowed one night of wallowing and feeling sorry for myself. Tomorrow would start with another pep talk and one phone call after another until I found a job.

~

"I got to the last round. This one's on you." Marcos was unfairly tough on me when I was trying to lick my wounds. The first beer went down easy, the liquid coating my parched throat. I'd spilled everything to Marcos, from the other contestants, to the judges, sleeping with Elle, her betrayal. Everything.

He'd stayed quiet, letting me spill my guts, like best friends do. While I flagged down our server and ordered another round of beers, he sat back, arms folded across his chest, and simply observed me.

"What?" I couldn't take it anymore. I needed some feedback. Some commiseration. Maybe a few comments about how Elle was the biggest bitch on the planet for dumping me and I could have any woman anywhere so who cares about her anyway.

Instead, he just smirked at me, reminding me an awful lot of

Elle, with his dark eyes and hair. "You went and fell in love with her, didn't you?"

The blood drained from my face and I picked up my beer for another sip, only to realize it was empty, which was why I'd ordered another round. "What?"

"You said that already." His grin grew and I felt the sudden urge to punch him in his stupid face. Let's see him get all the girls with a black eye and busted lip.

"Dude. What the fuck?" I splayed my hands out to the side. "We're here at a bar and I'm telling you what this woman did to me, your best friend, and that's what you say?"

"Yeah, exactly. I'm your best friend. I know you, asshole, so quit lying to me that she didn't mean anything to you. You're clearly more butthurt she betrayed you than the fact you lost the competition that could set your career on fire on national TV. It's pretty fucking obvious you love her."

The server set down our beers and left. I picked up the glass bottle and guzzled half of it, giving myself time to think. I thought about what I was most upset about. What part tore me up more than the rest? It was a hard question to answer when all I could see in my mind was Elle's beautiful face.

I slammed the beer down on the table. "Fucking-A. I hate it when you're right."

Marcos slapped me on the shoulder, like he was proud I'd finally stated the obvious. "So, what are you going to do about it?"

I scrunched up my face. "Do about what?"

He shook his head, exasperated. "My God, you're dense. What are you going to do about Elle?"

"There's nothing to do, dumbass. She doesn't want to be with me and she lives in New York. Not like we're going to accidentally run into each other on opposite coasts. Besides, she has her precious restaurant to open. She doesn't have time for me."

Marcos nodded slowly. "Okay, so get over her then."

I rolled my eyes. "Sure, yeah. No problem. I'll get right on that."

"Or..." Marcos lowered his voice and I couldn't help myself. I leaned in. "You could work your ass off getting your life in order and then go win her back." He hurried on when he saw my objections already bubbling up. "Hear me out. She didn't want to get involved with a contestant. Great, show's over. She didn't want to jeopardize her restaurant. Great, give her time to get it open and then go see her. Which gives you time to get your own job, get Abi back, and get your life in order too."

He opened his arms out wide to the side like he deserved a fucking medal for figuring out my whole life for me. But the truth of the matter was, I didn't know if I wanted to pursue things with Elle. I didn't know who she was. Not really. Was she the soft but sassy woman she'd shown me behind closed doors or was she the cold and calculating woman she'd been on other occasions?

"I agree with you on one thing. I need to get my life together as soon as possible. Everything else will have to wait. Maybe by the time I do that I'll have a better idea of what I want to do. Maybe this thing with Elle was just massive lust that I mistook for something else. I don't know and I can't take the time to worry about it right now. I need to save myself and my sister. No one else is gonna look out for us."

"Whatever you want to do, man. I support you no matter what you decide. The only thing I know for sure is I've never seen you torn up over a girl before. For whatever that's worth." Marcos tipped his beer to me and we clinked necks and drank it down.

A few beers later and I was starting to feel more settled. My chest still ached where my heart was supposed to be, but the beer and the conversation dulled the pain quite a bit. I had a plan and I was going full speed ahead with getting my life on track.

"I gotta head back to the apartment." Marcos waved our server over for the bill. "While you were gone, I crammed for the state real estate test and got my license."

"What? Why didn't you tell me? Instead of crying in my Cheerios, we could have been celebrating. Congrats, man." Marcos finished college same time I did with a business degree but still didn't know what he wanted to do. That is, until he'd randomly picked up a book about buying and selling properties at one of the few physical bookstores left on the planet.

He shrugged off my praise like it was nothing. "I've got an interview with a real estate team tomorrow down in San Francisco. If I can get on with them, it would be huge."

My smile faltered. "San Francisco, huh?"

He plastered on a grin, but wouldn't look at me. "Yeah, it would mean I had to move, but we'll see about all that later."

Jesus, growing up wasn't for the weak. "I'm happy for you, Marcos. Wherever life takes you."

We hugged it out like grown men did, with back slaps and grunts.

∼

"Hey, Michael, this is Austin Cox. Long time no talk, pal. Listen, I'm calling to see if you know of any friends looking for a chef. I'm applying for jobs and would love an introduction if you'd be willing."

I paced across the living room of my apartment at 9:00 a.m. the next morning placing phone calls to try to find a job. I was a man on a mission and even though Michael didn't sound like a guy I wanted to tangle with based on Elle's opinion, I was desperate. And desperate men will grovel.

"Austin. I'm surprised to hear from you. Didn't your buddy, Elle, get you hooked up?"

God, this guy was a greasy son of a bitch. "No, I haven't called her yet. Wouldn't say we're buddies."

"Huh." He let the silence hang there, maybe hoping I'd trip myself up and say more on the subject. "Well, sorry, buddy, but I don't know of any openings. I'll call you if I hear of anything, though. Good luck to you."

The line went dead and I stared at the phone in my hand. What a fucktard. I wouldn't hold my breath that I'd ever hear from him. Ah well, plenty of fish in the sea. Bertrand was next.

"Hi, Bertrand, this is Austin Cox. How are ya?"

"Austin! Lovely to hear from you. Are you missing everyone already? I sure am." The guy was a bow tie-wearing gem.

"Yeah, I'm having Taste Test withdrawals, for sure. Which is partly why I'm calling. Being on the show reinforced that cooking is my life's passion and I'd really like to get a job doing that. Do you know of anyone looking to hire a chef?"

"Hmm. I have to think for a second. Are you trying to stay in Northern California?"

"Honestly, I'd go anywhere, but I'll have my little sister with me, so I would hope it wouldn't be across the country."

"Okay, that helps. Lot more opportunity in Southern California. Let me talk to a couple people I know and then I'll call you right back. That work okay?"

Damn. He didn't even hesitate to help me out. "I would be most grateful, Bertrand. I really appreciate it."

"No problem, Austin. I really believe in your skills. Any restaurant would be lucky to have you."

While there were plenty of fish in the sea, I didn't know many of them. That was the extent of my calls. I didn't know anyone else in the business and there was no way I was going to call Elle and beg for a favor. I was desperate, but I didn't think filleting myself open and letting her pick at my innards was necessary at this point.

Instead, I fired up my computer and got busy looking at the want ads. Come hell or high water I'd be cooking for somebody by the end of the week. And the week after that? I'd get my sister back.

15
———

My apartment was exactly how I'd left it: cold, empty, and impersonal. I'd lived there for almost eight years and I had two pictures on my wall to show that a human being occupied the space. One of me in Greece, cooking on an old wood table and one of my mother and me on some guy's yacht off the coast of Italy. The man was long gone, just like all the others.

I had messages from both my executive chef and my building contractor with urgent questions for me. Prior to this trip, I would have been calling them back the minute my plane landed and I turned my cell phone back on while we taxied to the terminal. Somehow in the last two weeks, I'd lost my drive. The one that fueled my nonstop push for more. The one that ruled my life.

There was this weird pain in my chest. It felt like someone was sitting on me. I couldn't even take a full breath without wincing. I didn't recall bumping into anything hard enough to cause it, but it felt like I'd cracked a rib.

I threw my suitcase in my room and then moved to my living room to plop down on the white couch and gaze out at row upon row of apartments surrounding me. I could hear cars honking on the street below. The lady down the hall had her television turned up to concert level decibels. A teenager walked past my front door talking on his cell phone. There was evidence of people all around me.

And I was lonelier than I'd ever been.

I wanted to hear laughter. Get pulled into a warm bear hug. Maybe tease an old man about this lack of hair. Roll my eyes at a bleached blonde cheerleader host.

Without my consent, I'd somehow bonded with everyone on the set. I was back to the life I'd always wanted in New York and, somehow, I just wanted to go back to L.A. Back to people who enjoyed my company and didn't want anything from me. They simply accepted who I was and rolled with it.

My phone rang again and I slipped it out of my purse to see if it was either my chef or the building contractor. Seeing my mother's name flash on the screen had me pausing for a moment. I wasn't sure I was in the best frame of mind to deal with her right now. But if I didn't, she'd keep calling back. At least this way I could rush her off the phone saying I had calls to make.

"Hello, Mother."

"*¡Mi amor!* Are you back to civilization?" Her voice was already putting me on edge. She sounded happy to hear from me when just a few days ago we'd been arguing over her butting her nose in my business.

"Yes, Mother. I'm back at the apartment. I've got a lot of calls to make to get caught up. Opening day is in two weeks."

"Ah, well, it's a good thing you didn't hire Carl. Turned out to be a typical man. Not worth my time." She sniffed.

I rolled my eyes. "Yes, that's why I didn't want to hire him for my restaurant. Not a good idea to mix business with friends and family, you know?"

"Well, maybe if you'd given him a job he wouldn't have been so cold with me."

I shook my head, thoroughly annoyed. "Sure, whatever you say, Mother. Listen, I've gotta go and make those calls. Talk soon?"

"Oh, but wait! I was calling to let you know I won't be in town for your opening. I was invited to go with Paul on a cruise. I couldn't possibly turn that down." She trilled out a laugh on par with a paper cut.

The squeeze in my chest was more pronounced. "Mother, it's my big opening. My own restaurant, remember? You have to be there!"

"Don't be dramatic, darling. I'll come by and check out the place when I get back in town. Besides, Paul has some connections with a few magazines. Your old mother might still have it."

I took a deep breath and let it out, not at all surprised. Massive disappointment was a recurring theme in our relationship. "Okay. Good luck. Goodbye, Mother." I hung up without waiting for an answer. There was no point.

Slipping my heels off, I leaned over to lay my head on the armrest of the couch, my legs curled up next to me. I should have been calling my chef. I should have been heading down to the restaurant to see the new construction. There were a lot of things I should have been doing.

But for today, I was going to ignore it all and wallow. I had no one in my life who cared if I accomplished those things or not. I'd had a chance to have someone who cared, but I'd pushed him away in order to get my restaurant.

Growing up, I adored my mother with her pretty hair and fancy clothes, jetting around from one exotic location to another. But then the shine started to wear off with each school event she missed, each holiday we spent apart because she was too busy to come home. Then I started to catch on to the trail of boyfriends she brought in and out of our lives. The mean ones, the nice but boring ones, the slimy ones, the rich ones, and the ones who adored my mother but she dumped them when they no longer served her purposes. My mother was cold, only looking out for herself. She used people, including her own daughter.

Not unlike what I'd become.

Austin had accused me of being cold. I'd dashed his dreams in order to secure my own, which was the very definition of using someone and looking out for myself.

I was my mother.

And with that dark and ugly realization, I cried myself to sleep on the couch. Alone.

"We're just about finished with the tile in the bathrooms. From there, it's just installing light fixtures and getting your decorator in here." My construction contractor walked me through the space, my plans turned into a real, live restaurant. It was amazing to see the change they'd made in just two weeks while I was away. It helped that it had already been a restaurant when I bought the space, but we'd still had to move some things around to make it functional like I knew it needed to be.

I should be jumping up and down like Lindsey the effervescent host. I should be giddy with excitement at how well everything was coming together. Or hell, even sweating like poor Dale with nerves about opening night being so close. But all I could think about was how much I wanted to tell Austin every little detail and have him wrap me in one of his signature hugs.

I was coming out of my numbness. Anger at myself, anger at him, anger at the world in general was eating away at the despair I felt. Problem was, I liked the numbness. It was preferable over the guilt eating away at the edges of everything I did.

I twirled around to march back through the kitchen and force my brain to focus on what still needed to be done. Of course, I didn't see the box of paint sitting on the floor. Nor the paint bucket I kicked and knocked over.

My contractor jumped into action and righted it before more than a half-dollar size of gray paint spilled onto the new wood floors. He hollered and another guy came running in with wet towels to mop it up before it ruined anything.

I blew out a breath and shook out my hands. I needed to get my shit together before I ruined everything. *"Lo siento..."* I mumbled.

My contractor threw me a cautious look. He was probably scared to walk me through lest I wreak my havoc on anything else he'd just finished.

"Everything okay?" He looked like a guy about to stick his hand in a snake pit. Cautious and ready for things to get ugly.

I blew out another deep breath and willed the burning behind my eyes to cut that shit out. Nodding, I attempted a smile. He lurched back, eyes wide.

"Um, you have a little something..." He motioned toward his eye. I frowned and reached up to my own eye, not feeling anything. There was a mirror on the wall behind him, so I leaned closer to see what he was talking about, only to find my black winged eyeliner had traced a new line up on my eyelid, making me look batshit crazy. Great. Two weeks of a makeup artist and I'd forgotten how to do my own makeup. I tried to scrub the line off my lid, but succeeded only in making it look like dark eyeshadow. Today's look was emo apparently.

As if my failed makeup was the straw that broke the camel's back, the burning behind my eyes intensified to the point I could no longer out-breathe it. I spun in my contractor's direction and wrapped my arms around his waist.

He stiffened and kept his hands out to the side, refusing to touch me.

"I'm just having a hard time right now, you know?" I sniffled into his chest. When I realized he wasn't hugging me back, it made me think of Austin and how this must have been how I acted when he tried to hug me. That made me cry harder.

He started walking backward, one faltering step after another. Still, I didn't unlock my arms, just shuffled after him, burrowing my face into his chest harder. I needed a hug, goddammit.

"Ms. Fierro. You must let go. I have work to do. Please."

His quivering voice broke me out of whatever parallel universe I was in. I was hugging strange men, forcing them to give me comfort. What brand of crazy had I become?

I immediately released him, my face blazing. I couldn't look at him, instead studying the floor like the psychotherapy drugs I needed would suddenly appear there.

"*Lo siento,* I'm so sorry..." I grabbed my handbag and left in a hurry, breathing in muggy New York air on the sidewalk like I'd run a marathon.

Out of nowhere, a black cat came around the side of the building and walked right in front of me, rubbing against my leg like he was trying to scrape off bad luck. For the love of all things holy, today was not my day, fate was not on my side, and the universe was conspiring against me. I wasn't as superstitious as my mother, but a black cat in the middle of the concrete jungle? I'd take it as the sign that it was.

With people rushing by me in every direction, I stood stock-still, coming to terms with my life. I needed to make things right. I needed to quit being like Mother. I wouldn't be her. Couldn't live the rest of my life like her. And the only one who could stop that eventuality was me.

Without giving my doubts a chance to rear their ugly heads, I pulled out my cell phone and dialed my old friend, Jon Paul, from culinary school. He was an interesting man and I was sad to say I hadn't kept up with him all that much since we graduated and went our separate ways. Hopefully he'd still remember me.

"Jon Paul? It's Elle Fierro. How are you?"

There was a slight pause during which I physically cringed

over not being a better friend. "The infamous El Jefe is calling me? To what do I owe the honor, my dear?"

Oh, thank God, he remembered me.

"Well. To be honest, I have an opportunity for you, but first, I need to apologize."

"This sounds interesting. Do go on." He sounded like he was trying not to laugh.

"Yes. I need to apologize for not being a better friend. It's come to my attention that I may not be the best at reaching out. Not super warm and friendly, you could say."

At that, he burst out laughing, the giant belly laugh a little over the top if you asked me. I was trying to apologize and here he was laughing at me. The black cat kept rubbing itself on my leg, much to my irritation.

"Oh, Elle, I'm sorry. I don't mean to laugh at you, but that's an understatement if I've ever heard one. I love you, girl, but warm and cuddly you're not."

It stung a little to hear his honest opinion. I figured I deserved it, though. Maybe if I was slapped in the face with it enough I'd learn my lesson. It was sounding more and more like I'd been on the path to becoming my mother for quite some time.

"Yeah, so I've heard. I'm sorry. Really, Jon Paul. You were my closest friend in culinary school and I've neglected to keep in touch since. For what it's worth, I really regret that. And if you'll let me, I'd like to be a better friend now. In the future. Well, all the time." I quit talking, needing to gauge his reaction to know if the sentiment was coming out right. I'd never tried to apologize like this or make someone be a friend of mine again, so I could have been going about the whole thing wrong.

His voice was soft. "Elle. Thank you for apologizing, but it's okay. I've met your mother, remember? I get it. And I'm happy to be your friend. Now, in the future, and all the time. We're good, honey."

The pain in my ribs eased a bit and I took a full breath.

"Thank you." The black cat quit using me as a scratching post and sauntered off to find a new victim. I just hoped it stayed out of the street.

"So, what's the opportunity?"

I smiled, feeling slightly better now that I was making amends. My heart was still crushed knowing Austin was gone forever, but releasing myself from the guilt over my involvement in his disappointment was underway and that felt good. "I know an incredible new, young chef looking for a job. He's going to be a household name, I guarantee it. And you can be the one to mentor him. I don't want him knowing I pulled the strings, but you'd be a fool not to hire him."

Jon Paul only paused for a second. "Wow, I've never heard you sing anyone's praises before, so this guy must be the real deal. I actually do need a chef for a new restaurant I'm opening in Santa Monica next month. I have a few candidates already, but I'm happy to include your guy in the interview process."

"Excellent, thank you. Just remember to keep my name out of it, okay?"

"You got it, Elle."

16

———

ustin

I unbuttoned the top button of my dress shirt and ripped the tie off my neck, throwing it into the car. It was hotter than balls already this early in the day. Sinking into the driver's seat, I scrubbed a hand over my face. Goddamn, that was an awful interview.

As I waited for Bertrand to get back to me, I'd applied for several jobs at local restaurants with several call backs. The pickings were slim, but desperate times and all that. I'd pulled into the parking lot of the first restaurant full of hope this morning, only to see the signage to the restaurant had changed, one letter not lighting up as it should. It was an unfortunate electrical error that had me interviewing at Black Anus this morning. If that wasn't a sign of my current status, I didn't know what was.

I'd gone from Hollywood reality star to interviewing as a kitchen assistant for a rectally challenged steakhouse.

I had another interview that afternoon at a Red Lobster,

146

which I knew if I got, would just about kill Abi, seeing as how I'd be frying up cute little shrimp all day long. Maybe I could convince the restaurant to put my squid recipe on the menu. Although I doubted they rewarded creativity in the kitchen. More like get it out fast and cooked all the way through so no one gets sick.

My cell phone rang while I was driving, a number I didn't recognize. Hoping it was Bertrand calling me back, or maybe one of his associates, I pulled over and took the call, my heart hammering in my chest.

"Austin Cox speaking."

"Hello, Austin, this is Chef Jon Paul. How are you?"

"Good, thank you. What can I do for you?"

"I was given your name, and once I put in a few calls to find out about you, I decided I couldn't waste another minute before giving you a call. I have a restaurant opening in Santa Monica next month and I need a sous chef. The job is yours if you want it."

A huge truck whizzed by me and rocked my little car on the side of the road. I wasn't sure I heard the man correctly. It sounded like he was offering me a job on the spot. He must have taken my silence as hesitation because after a pause, he kept talking.

"The cuisine is a nice California fusion, but we're still nailing down the menu offerings. If I get you on board fast enough, you can collaborate with my executive chef to get some say in it. I have a nice salary package I can send over via email if you'd like to take a look before making a decision. But I would need you in the area as soon as possible. What do you say?"

"I-I say thank you! Yes. I'd love to come work for you."

"Excellent! Why don't you give me your email. I'll send you further information and then call me when you think you'll be in town and able to start." Jon Paul wasn't messing around.

"That sounds wonderful. Thank you so much."

We ended the call soon after and I sat for quite a while, trying to come to terms with what just happened. My mind was scrambling with all that had to be done. I needed to get out of my apartment lease, pack all my stuff, find a place in Santa Monica, petition the court for guardianship.

Oh, and find a way to grab that ol' bastard Bertrand by the lapels and give him a kiss on his shiny almost-bald head. He'd come through for me in an incredibly short period of time. He was my new best friend and didn't know it yet.

I immediately ached to call Elle and tell her she'd been right. I did have talent, just like she said, and I could make my passion my career. I flipped my phone over and over in my hands, debating whether to call her. In the end, I put my phone in the glovebox to prevent falling for the temptation in a moment of weakness. She wanted nothing to do with me. I had to let her go.

So with hope dancing in my chest where my heart had been, I drove home to break the news to Marcos. Things were finally looking up.

～

Two Weeks Later

"I'd like to propose a toast." I lifted my beer in the air and waited for Marcos and Abi to join me. When their glasses joined mine, I continued. "To new beginnings, to our future successes, and to always being family no matter where we live."

"Hear, hear!" Marcos replied whole-heartedly.

"No matter what," Abi whispered, tears in her eyes as she took a sip of her soda.

Thankfully, they were happy tears now. Today was my first official day as her guardian. The court had quickly granted me guardianship when I submitted my hiring papers, along with a copy of the new lease I had on a two-bedroom apartment in Santa Monica, right off the 10 freeway. It wasn't fancy, by any means, what with the view of Southern California traffic, but it was a start. We'd be together and that's what mattered most.

Marcos had gotten the job at the real estate firm in San Francisco, so he was moving tomorrow as well. It was sad to see our apartment all packed up, considering we'd been roommates since we left the dorms at nineteen. This was simply our time to grow up and move on. We both had promising careers ahead of us and lives to build.

"I can't believe we're all splitting up." Abi, out of all of us, had the most to be sad about. While I'd miss Marcos like a phantom limb, I had the excitement of my career taking off to distract me. Abi would be saying goodbye to Marcos—he'd been like an older brother to her growing up—our mom had just passed away, and now I was taking her away from the only town she knew along with all her friends. But in true Abi form, she pulled herself up out of the dumps and looked at the bright side. "Hey, at least I'll be in smog and traffic for the last two years of my childhood." She crossed her eyes and stuck her tongue out at me.

Marcos jumped in and beat me to it. "Hey, just don't get messed up in those SoCal boys. Don't be won over by their surfboards and floppy blond hair."

"Don't worry. I have locks on her windows," I joked.

Abi pouted, but didn't look very upset. She'd gone to some high school dances with dates, but hadn't had a boyfriend yet. I'm sure that would be a barrel of laughs when we crossed that road.

After we gave our orders to the server. I got their attention and got serious. "I meant my toast, you two. We're family. No matter where we live, let's make a pact to remain tight. You with me?"

Marcos clapped me on the shoulder. "Don't worry. Brothers for life."

Abi sighed dramatically. "Ah, such a beautiful bromance."

"Shut up, Abilene, you're stuck with us."

Abi beamed right back at me and all was right with my world.

Well, except for the fact I'd gone numb in that empty space in my chest where my heart used to beat. I'm sure that wasn't healthy, but I'd take it over the crushing pain I felt when Elle first walked away from me.

I'd dreamed about her almost every night the last two weeks, which was both a heaven and hell. Considering we were on opposite ends of the country, the nightly visit made me feel like she was still next to me, her scent and her lips still ghosting across my skin in the middle of the night. Then I'd wake up and hell would begin as my brain realized she was gone, nothing but elusive fragments of an overactive imagination.

So, numbness I'd take. It would have to do until I could figure out how to get over her entirely. The job, the move, and getting custody of my sister had been a nice distraction. When that all became the new norm, then I'd address matters of the heart. I couldn't be TinMan forever.

The move to Santa Monica was remarkably uneventful. Between Abi and me we didn't have a whole lot of stuff. When Mom died, we went through all her things and kept what we wanted as keepsakes, the rest donated to the local shelter. One small truckload and my car were all we needed as we trekked down the coast to our new home.

We put away the essentials in our respective bedroom closets and in the tiny kitchen. We were unpacked in time to eat takeout Chinese on the living room floor and talk about what we needed to still buy for the place. First on both our lists was a television. The one at my old place had been Marcos' and I could see how much of a priority that would be.

Abi was still on summer break, which gave me time to get her registered at the closest public high school. She was still sleeping the next morning when I had to leave to meet Jon Paul at the new restaurant space. I left her a note on the kitchen counter to keep unpacking and make a list of what else we needed, and then off I went. Thankfully, Santa Monica was a fairly sleepy part of L.A. and I didn't get lost or need a smartphone with a map. And of course, my brain went straight to the days I navigated using Elle's phone. She was probably right. I did need to upgrade my phone.

"Nope, not bringing her with me to my new job. Today is about new beginnings." It was also apparently a day for pep talks out loud in the car. I knew where my thoughts had been the last two weeks and they were on a downward spiral into the shitter when I thought about how she hadn't even reached out to me. She'd walked off that set without a backward glance or a "fuck you later." I would never understand how she could have warm blood beating through her veins and do that.

I pulled alongside the curb of a side street that connected right to Pacific Coast Highway. I hopped out and the view stopped me in my tracks. As far as the eye could see was solid blue Pacific Ocean. Even the air there was different. Cleaner, cooler, the kind that made you want to suck in lungfuls of it and close your eyes, savoring it.

Instead I looked up and saw the newly installed iron sign *Rustic Water* over the giant bifolding glass doors. This was it. My new home away from home.

I walked through and saw people moving about in the back. "Hello?" I called out as I approached.

A very large man spun around and walked over, hand outstretched, his face mostly a giant smile with tiny eyes reduced to slits with the fullness of his cheeks trying to touch his forehead. "Hello! You must be Austin. I'm Jon Paul."

I liked him instantly. "Nice to meet you, Jon Paul. Thank you so much for inviting me to be a part of your beautiful restaurant."

His big hand swiped through the air, narrowly dodging my

face. "No, no. The honor is all mine. Let me show you around and when my executive chef arrives, you two can sit and get the menu finalized. I have the final say, but you and he will build it. It's good to be the boss, no?" His eyes twinkled and he looked ready to chuckle.

He gave me a tour of the kitchen, which was state of the art from the kitchen towels thicker than my bath towels to the specialty ovens made for hearth-fired pizzas. Everything was set up to be extremely functional and big enough for everyone in the kitchen to flow together even on the busiest of nights. The dining area was gorgeous in a sleek, modern California way. Tables along the side of the restaurant all had an ocean view, which would draw people in, even if the food sucked, which it wouldn't if I had anything to say about it. And guess what? I was the sous chef, so I definitely had a say in it.

By the time the tour was over, Jon Paul was able to introduce me to the executive chef he'd hired. Before Jon Paul could break away and attend to everything else that needed to be done before opening, I shook his hand again and thanked him for the job.

"No thanks needed. Just do a killer job for me, that's all I ask."

"You bet I will. Make sure you let Bertrand know how thankful I am for the introduction." I'd left Bertrand a message with my sincere thanks, but hadn't gotten a phone call back, which as I thought about it, was quite odd. I'd been so busy moving, I hadn't pressed the issue.

Jon Paul looked confused. "Bertrand Paul? How is that old goat?"

Now I was confused. "He's good. But didn't you two just talk?"

"No. I haven't seen him in a few years. He still doing that crazy comb-over?"

I nodded, in a bit of a daze. Jon Paul laughed and walked away shaking his head. If Bertrand didn't get me this job, then who did? Michael Fin?

There was no way. That man was a total bottom feeder and wouldn't help his mother, let alone me.

The question swam through my brain as I tried to concentrate on my conversation with the new executive chef. We spent three hours hammering out the details of the menu. I was shocked he listened to me and implemented some of my ideas.

But mostly, I listened and absorbed, wanting to learn everything this man could teach me. I was an untried newbie. I had to show both him and Jon Paul that I could be trusted. The first way to do that was to be a team player, someone they could count on. I didn't have much experience and I'm sure it was safe to say most people in the industry wouldn't take a chance on someone like me. Either Jon Paul was particularly trusting or someone had really put in a good word. But my mom taught me never to look a gift horse in the mouth. I didn't care how I got it. It was mine and I was going to rock that kitchen.

As I left the restaurant, I reminded myself that my only focus beyond my sister was this restaurant and this opportunity. If I couldn't have Elle—and it was becoming crystal clear I couldn't —then I would devote myself to my career and my sister.

Maybe one day, a long way into the future, I'd patch together a new heart that could beat again for someone else. Not now, not any time soon, and definitely not for Elle.

17

Elle

"Deep breaths. Just remember to breathe," I muttered to myself as I smoothed down my deep burgundy dress. Today was my grand opening. The day my restaurant was open for business. The day all my dreams would come to fruition.

My staff was ready, the space was ready, the critics were about to walk in the door, the press had already been by with their cameras and their interview questions. All that was left was for me to give the signal and the night would begin. My hands were shaking as I checked my makeup one last time in the mirror in the back where my staff stored all their personal belongings.

"Now's not the time to go soft. Everything you've ever wanted is right here, right now. You're going to go out there and smile like you're the happiest woman in New York." I gave myself a pep talk, one that was badly needed. I'd been going through the motions the last few weeks, doing what needed to be done to get this place open, but my heart was oddly not in it.

I couldn't seem to get my thoughts away from Austin. I'd made the phone call to Jon Paul to assuage my guilt and to do the right thing.

I should have felt better. I should have been able to let Austin go. But if anything, he'd haunted my thoughts even more. I was in an Austin-induced funk and I didn't know how to get out.

"El Jefe, you ready?" My executive chef popped his head in the room, the concern clear on his face. I was already five minutes late and that was very unlike me.

Forcing a broad smile on my face, I nodded and followed him out of the room, through the kitchen, and into the dining area. The maître d' looked at me for the go-ahead.

One last deep breath and I bowed my head. My staff jumped into action and the doors to my restaurant opened for my first guests. The rest of the night was a blur of handshakes, kisses on the cheek, and softly spoken words to each diner as I made my way through the tables. My head pounded from holding the smile that should have come naturally. My feet protested my sky-high heels and my chest ached for Austin to whisper in my ear to take them off and get comfortable.

The one thing that stood out the most from my night was that Mother and Austin weren't in attendance. My mother because she just didn't care, and Austin because I had been the one to push him away like I didn't care.

One day blurred into the next. I read glowing reviews in the paper and online about my new restaurant. I smiled for pictures and thanked my staff profusely every night for a job well done. I shook hands and turned away more men just like the hot Italian from what felt like so long ago.

Nothing lit me up and set my spirit on fire.

I was dead inside.

So two weeks after my restaurant opened, I sat on my white couch in the dark after a long night of working, a huge glass of a full-bodied merlot in my hand. And I made a decision. One I would have never even considered in the past. I was going to take a vacation, leaving my restaurant in the capable hands of my executive chef.

I was going to Los Angeles.

I was going to talk to Austin and see where things were between us.

I was probably crazy.

But I was about to crawl out of my own skin, I was so tired of living a passionless life. I wasn't yelling at my staff like I normally would. They didn't even flinch when I walked through the kitchen. It was a disgrace. *I* was a disgrace.

Nothing seemed to penetrate this heavy blanket of sadness I was carrying around every day. I went to work, I came home, I went to sleep. Repeat. Thriving on that schedule was easy before, but now I could barely stand myself.

Where was the conversation? The teasing? The laughter? Austin had exposed me to so much more and now I couldn't seem to live without it. I wanted hugs, and food fights, and him by my side while I navigated...well, everything.

As each sip of wine slid down my throat faster and my plan formed in more detail, I started to get angry. Just a tiny spark that lit up my brain and stirred something in my gut. How dare he push his way into my life and make me indifferent about every-thing I used to love? I'd rather hate my life than be lukewarm about it. Lukewarm was for losers who never amounted to anything in life because they just went with the flow without any clear opinion about anything. Dear God, let me hate or love it, but not that bullshit in between.

I was going to Los Angeles and Austin and I would talk. We'd get to the bottom of whatever was going on between us. We'd see if it was as dead as my feelings for my life or if I'd simply left my fire there with him. He probably hated me by now, so the whole thing might go up in flames, but I'd rather it all burn to the ground than stay where I was.

~

Two days later, I slid into a black dress, the lack of color the perfect symbol for what my life had become. I was in a small hotel two blocks away from where Austin was working. I'd driven by Rustic Water on my way from the airport last night and it was beautiful, situated right by the coastline, a warm and friendly look to it that seemed popular based on the number of people outside waiting for their table.

I'd felt a strong pull to park and try to catch a glimpse of him, or even to sit outside the building to just be closer to Austin, but even in my addled brain that sounded borderline crazy. Better to get to my hotel, check in, get some sleep, and plan my attack the next day.

So there I was putting on my battle armor, the slinkiest black dress I owned, my makeup on point, my hair down, and the most ridiculous shoes I owned. It didn't escape my notice that no version of myself would ever do this unless I was in love. Which made my move this evening even more important to get right. How could I have fallen in love with Austin then betrayed him and walked away for a month? That was actually an easy question.

I'd been raised by a mother who didn't understand what true love was, so how could she have taught me? A goddamn cupid in a white diaper could have flown right in front of me and hit me with an arrow and I wouldn't have known it was love. I was floating in uncharted waters, flailing around with one oar and no sense of direction. I'd either be rescued by a hot seaman or drown all by myself. There was no telling.

In the worst plan in history, I decided to walk the two blocks to the restaurant, which would have been easy in normal shoes. In my stilettos I nearly broke an ankle and surely strained the tiny muscles that ran along the bottom of my feet. It was all worth it, though, when I joined the throng of people waiting to get in and I saw male heads turning to check me out. That sounded conceited, but I didn't actually care about their attention. All I wanted was for one particularly shaggy-haired head to turn in my direction.

I was seated right on time at a little table for two. Yes, I'd called ahead to get a reservation—this was my grand plan, after all. I ordered a glass of red wine to calm my nerves and perused the menu like a starving woman. My nervous stomach probably wouldn't let me eat more than a few bites, but I was hungry for any information on how Austin was doing.

I pulled in a quick breath when I read a menu item for squid, the description very similar to the dish Austin had made during the filming of Taste Test. That had to have been his addition to the menu. The coincidence was too great.

When my server came back for my order, I made sure to get the squid, needing to eat the dish Austin had made. If his hands made it, I wanted it in my mouth. I strained my neck trying to see into the kitchen every time a person came from the back, but it was never Austin. While I waited for my food I started to get nervous again, chastising myself for not calling Jon Paul ahead of time and making sure Austin was working tonight. This whole plan wouldn't work if he wasn't here.

Then my food was set in front of me and the smell was divine. Seeing his food on the fancy table in front of me, the diners all around me enjoying things he helped create was doing weird things to my heart. I was bursting with pride. He'd made his dreams come true, no thanks to me.

Taste Test was set to release our premiere episode tomorrow. Commercials had already been running and it was beyond bizarre to see myself on television. It was a special kind of hell to see Austin and not be with him. Between that series starting to air and his success at Rustic Water, Austin's career would soon be exploding. Maybe talking to him now about how I felt would only be a distraction he didn't need.

But as I put that first bite of food in my mouth I was thrown back to our days on set. Like people getting nostalgic over a song from their youth, that burst of flavor immediately took me back to how I felt when things were good with Austin and me. How alive I felt. How cared for and adored. How he listened to me and genuinely wanted to know how my day went. How he teased me and made me laugh.

I couldn't walk away again without trying. I just couldn't.

"Miss?" I flagged down my server. She came over with a confused smile. "I'm so sorry, but this squid dish is all wrong."

She gave her head a quick shake like she couldn't believe what she was hearing. "I-I'm so sorry, ma'am. Let me take it back and get you a new one."

I nodded, sorry to run this little charade, but needing a way in. "Thank you, I really appreciate that."

She whisked the plate away and hurried into the back. My heart was in my throat, beating out a fast rhythm hummingbirds would envy. She was back in a matter of minutes, a new steamy dish in her hands.

"Here you go. Please let me know if this is to your liking." She placed the food in front of me and then backed away to wring her hands.

I picked up my fork and speared a circle of squid, placing it carefully in my mouth. I chewed slowly and even though it was beyond delicious, I scrunched up my nose. "No. I'm sorry. It's not going to work. The texture is not right. Take it back."

The server looked well and truly alarmed by then, whisking the plate away again and practically running to the kitchen. She came back, a look of dread on her face. I sniffed, sat up straighter, and took another bite. I set my fork down as I chewed and clenched my fist under the table to get through what I had to do.

"No. I must speak to your chef."

To her credit, she handled the difficult situation well. She nodded and asked if I could follow her. I scraped my chair back and set my napkin next to my third plate of the best squid dish I'd ever had. My focus momentarily shifted to simply walking in my stilettos and not embarrassing myself in front of a room full of people. My plan couldn't come to fruition if I went down before I made it to the kitchen.

I found myself in a cramped office space with a messy desk and a calendar on the wall with appointments circled and crossed out. The server asked me to wait for just a moment before she slipped out to check on diners who were far less difficult than me. Clasping my hands behind my back, I waited and reminded myself to breathe.

What felt like years later, but was probably only minutes, the door burst open and in walked everything that mattered to me. His hair was disheveled, like he'd run his hand through it one too many times that night. But his chef's whites looked incredible on him, like he was born to wear them.

His eyes flew down my body and then back up to my face. He stumbled back a step and I lurched forward. If he was going to run from the room, I had to get a head start to stop him what with these damn shoes.

"Austin—" I reached out to touch his arm. He flinched and I let my hand drop down to my side, dejected.

"I should have known it was you sending back my signature dish. That squid is fucking perfect. There's no way someone would send it back." His voice was delicious, tickling my senses and easing the craving I'd had for weeks.

I shrugged, acting casual, though I was anything but. If anything I was bursting with pride that he believed in himself. He was finally confident in his abilities and he wore it like a sexy layer. "I was always a little difficult."

He made a noise in his throat that could have been agreement. "What are you doing here, Elle?"

I closed my eyes for a moment, enjoying the way he said my

name. Opening them again, I drank in the sight of him, wondering if this glimpse would have to last me a lifetime.

"I'm so sorry, Austin." He folded his arms across his chest and I rushed to get the rest out. "I'm sorry for betraying you. I'm sorry for not understanding the gift of what we had. I'm so damn sorry for not being who you deserved. I've realized these last few weeks that all the things I thought I cared about don't really mean much after all. I've gotten quite a few things wrong, but there's just one thing I'd like to get right."

"Elle." His jaw clenched. "I don't have time for this now. I'm in the middle of dinner service." His hands went to his hair and he raked his fingers through before finishing his thought. "Look, come by later if you want and we'll talk. But I can't do this right now, okay?"

"That's fair." I nodded, beyond excited he'd given me an opening. "What time do you get off tonight?"

"Not until one in the morning. Sure you can wait around?" He sounded like he expected me to bail the minute things weren't the way I wanted. He was going to have to meet the new Elle, the one who compromised for the people she loved.

"I'll meet you at one o'clock outside."

I had a squid dish to finish and flats to change into. Then I'd settle in for the night and wait for my chance.

18

ustin

What the fuck was happening?

First I had an angry customer on my hands saying my squid dish wasn't up to par, which was total bullshit. That dish was the seafood bomb. Then the angry customer turned out to be Elle, looking more beautiful than any of the many renditions from my dreams.

And she was sorry?

I was stuck in a Dr. Jekyll and Mr. Hyde play where too-hot-to-handle Elle came out to tease me and then disappeared behind the icy, elusive facade of El Jefe. Tonight, it appeared I was dealing with Elle, which was almost the worst choice of the pair. Elle had the ability to rip my slowly repairing heart to shreds, whereas El Jefe would just reinforce why I was also busy building a fragile wall around my heart.

If I could make it the next few hours without burning myself or food poisoning my guests, I'd count myself lucky. My brain was focused solely on Elle and what this visit could mean. I absolutely hated that a huge part of me was already excited, leaping over all our problems to land in Giddysville where we could just pick up where we left off before she imploded my world.

When the clock struck one, I hung up my chef's coat and splashed water on my face. The rest of the staff would finish the cleanup and I'd never wished to join them after a busy night. Now that the time was here, I was dreading this conversation with Elle. I mean, she might not even show up. El Jefe never waited for anyone.

With my keys twirling around my finger, I stepped out of the back door of the restaurant and nearly shit my pants when Elle jumped into my path, her stature several inches shorter than normal.

I grabbed my chest and stumbled back. "Jesus, Elle. Don't jump out at people in a dark alley like that."

She bit her lip sheepishly and I nearly came in my pants on the spot. My poor pants would need a good washing before the night was over.

"Sorry. I just wanted to make sure you saw me."

I frowned. "Why are you so short?"

Her eyes widened and she smacked me on the stomach, the tallest body part she could reach from way down there. "Hey! Don't make fun of short people. That's not nice."

I squinted down and in the dark light could just make out that she wore flip-flops. "You own flip-flops?"

She sighed loudly. "I do now. Just bought a pair down the street. They're really comfortable."

"Yeah, I know. So are Vans and Converse and Toms. All shoes you've probably never had the pleasure of wearing since they're flats."

She rolled her eyes, but the side of her mouth tipped up. "Believe it or not I didn't fly all the way over here to discuss my footwear."

I grabbed her arm and tugged her with me as I walked toward the beach. There was a little bench right underneath a streetlight I'd become good friends with since working at *Rustic Water*. Nearly every night after work I'd sit for a few minutes to an hour, contemplating life and just taking in the ocean. The sound of the waves and the rhythm to it was soothing in a way I needed.

No one was around this late at night, so even with the yellow light from the bulb overhead, it felt like we were in our own little bubble, the Pacific Ocean the only witness to whatever would be said in this charged conversation.

I sat first and she sank into the bench next to me, a couple inches of space between us. I could smell her perfume, its scent bringing back memories of skimming my face along her skin, inhaling as much of her as I could with the short time we had together.

"I should start this thing off since I was the one to walk away in the first place." Elle was looking right at me, her tone begging for me to understand.

I refused to look at her, instead pretending to find the ocean fascinating. There was no way I'd take the chance of looking at her. I could already feel myself softening to her with just the small banter in the alley outside the restaurant. The woman was too beautiful to stay mad at, and I had to hold onto that anger. What she did was wrong and I couldn't just overlook it because I wanted to sink my hands into her hair and bite that lip that was practically begging for my attention.

Her hand landed lightly on my forearm and my heart sped up just at the slight touch. I gritted my teeth and took a deep breath to stay focused.

"I wish I could give you a good reason for why I didn't pick you at the studio. I was feeling guilty for sleeping with a contestant, yes, but mostly I wanted to make sure Michael understood that nothing was going on between us. If I voted for you, I was afraid he'd tell everyone about us and both our reputations would be ruined."

I scrunched up my face, my anger flaring. "Please. No one knows who I am. At least be honest with me now. You were concerned about *your* reputation."

Out of the corner of my eye, I saw her flinch. "Yes. Yes, you're right of course. I was worried that everything I'd worked for and dreamed of was going to go away. So, I made my choice. And I went home and realized my dream and I'm still miserable. *Dios mío*, I cried on my contractor and tried to get him to hug me, I was so lonely. My own mother abandoned me on my opening night to hang with some new boy toy and I had absolutely no one to celebrate this huge thing with! It means nothing, Austin. Nothing!"

I turned and looked at her then, seeing tears in her eyes as she hopped off the bench to pace in front of me. "I had passion before. I was strict, my staff feared me, but they respected me too, you know? Now I have nothing. No passion. I don't give a shit about anything. Nothing motivates me, nothing matters." She threw her hands in the air and faced me. "I messed up, Austin. I made the wrong choice. I'm sorry."

Her sorrow hit me like a wall. I'd been so hell-bent on protecting myself from her that I hadn't seen the bags under her eyes, or the way her dress was absolutely gorgeous on her, but a bit on the baggy side. She didn't look right. She didn't look happy.

I nodded once. "Forgiven."

She did a double take. "What?"

I spoke slower. "You're forgiven."

Next thing I knew she'd rushed forward and wrapped her arms around my neck, squeezing the life out of me. I don't know who taught her how to hug, but she'd learned real quick.

"Thank you, Austin," she whispered in my ear. Then she nipped my earlobe with her teeth and I jerked back as I felt it like a shock all the way to my toes.

Her arms still clung to my neck, but we were face-to-face now.

Her eyes were wide and she held perfectly still. The moment extended, just the two of us staring at each other with the ocean waves the only sound. My heart was beating triple time like I'd run all the way to New York to find this woman. I wrestled with what I wanted.

I mean, there was a beautiful woman in front of me willing to give me her body, of that I was pretty sure. So that was a no-brainer. But this thing between us couldn't be casual. It couldn't be just another epic night in bed and the next day she'd turn her back on me. It would crush me this time. So, yeah, I wrestled with whether I should give in to the look she was giving me.

"Elle..." I half moaned. Her dark eyes sparkled back at me, an inky pool I could get lost in forever, if I wasn't careful.

"Austin," she whispered back. Then she swiveled and sat on my lap, my hands going to her hips without thought. "I don't know what love is, not really. But I know I've never felt this way about anyone before. I want one more hug with you more than I care about my reputation. I want to tease you again about your dinosaur phone rather than be at my restaurant. I want to ask you about your day, every day. I want passion back in my life and I think—no, I *know*—that you're the key."

I pressed my forehead to hers, absorbing everything she was saying. Because from where I was sitting, it sounded a lot like she felt the same way I did. Which had to mean I was dreaming. Did I fall asleep on the park bench like a homeless guy, dreaming of the woman I could never have?

"Austin?"

I blinked and Elle was still there, though she was looking a little pale.

"What I'm trying to say is I love you, Austin."

My heart stuttered.

"Could you pinch me, please?" I asked her.

Her nose scrunched up. "What?"

"Pinch me."

She tilted her head to the side, but reached down and pinched my thigh, none too gentle I might add.

I yelped accusingly, "Ouch!"

"You told me to pinch you, *¡tonto del culo!*"

"Hey, no need to call me names. I just wanted to make sure I wasn't dreaming."

She went to stand up. "Well, this isn't how I saw this going down."

I moved quickly to grab her by the waist, pulling her back onto my lap and nuzzling her neck. "I gotta say, El Jefe, I didn't see it going down this way either. I've never had a woman tell me she loved me in the same breath as calling me a dumbass." A chuckle escaped, and then a few more. Leave it to Elle to insult me right after she shared her love with me.

She smacked my chest, but smiled. Then she started giggling with me. We were just two lonely people finding each other again and laughing it out at two in the morning on a bench by the ocean.

When I could contain myself, I finally sank my hands into her hair and pulled her gorgeous face to me. Looking her in the eye, I whispered, "For what it's worth, I love you too, Elle." And then I nibbled on that lip before pillaging her mouth to make up for lost time.

The door slammed shut behind me, but I barely heard it as I banged into the wall. Elle was climbing me like a redwood, her little body surprisingly strong. She pulled at my shirt, a button popping off and flying under the bed, never to be found.

We'd made it back to her hotel with little issue. However, the minute the elevator doors closed, she'd turned into a crazy woman, her nails gripping me like she was afraid I'd disappear on her. Now that we had privacy, I gave as good as I got, ripping her dress over her head and tossing it aside.

I raised my fist to my mouth and backed up, taking her all in. She arched one dark eyebrow and slowly backed away. "You wanna see more?"

The temperature in the hotel room rocketed twenty degrees north and I bit my knuckle.

She reached behind her and unclasped her bra, tossing it onto the bedside lamp, which tipped, wobbled, and fell over. Neither of us even looked to assess the damage. I could buy a new lamp. I'd buy ten lamps. But I wasn't looking away from this woman for the rest of the night. Maybe the rest of my life.

Her thumbs shimmied her lacy panties down her hips and down her legs, kicking the offensive material under the bed, to live a wonderful life with my button.

Goddamn, she was the most stunning woman to ever live. It was easy to see her mother was a model, though Elle didn't get the height. Her features were the kind that sold millions of copies around the world. Hell, she could have quit cooking and become a lip model for some makeup company extolling the virtues of their long-lasting lip color.

And yet she loved me.

I quickly undressed and approached, our gazes locked, but I veered at the last second and lay down on the bed, my back against the headboard. "Come here."

She climbed on and straddled my lap, her arms on my shoulders. I laid my hands on the tops of her thighs, itching to go everywhere, explore every inch of her body. "Say it again," I whispered.

She smiled that relaxed smile, the one I was addicted to. It was just for me, that upturn of her lips, the eyes half closed. No one else got to see her like this. No one else knew she had this side to her. "I love you, Austin Cox."

My hands skimmed higher, my thumbs settling into the notch

where her thighs met. "I told you Team FieryCox was a winner." One thumb stroked up the middle, a gasp leaving her mouth. "Was I right?"

She nodded, her hair tumbling forward to block my view of her breasts.

I tsked. "Nuh-uh, I want to hear you say it." My thumb swiped again.

"Okay," she breathed. "Team FieryCox all the way, baby."

Now I was grinning. "See? That wasn't so hard to admit."

"Shut up. *Quiero hacerte el amor.*" She kissed the side of my grin, then the other. "*El hoyuelo,*" she mumbled.

I'd have to get her to translate later, but for now we'd communicate in a language we both understood. I cupped her jaw and captured her mouth, tangling our tongues while my thumb kept up a steady strumming. When she was rocking against me and more Spanish I didn't recognize was coming out of that mouth, I lifted her up and let her slide back down, impaled in her glorious body.

Forehead to forehead, we never broke eye contact as her hips undulated. I watched each twitch of her face, the way her eyes would widen as she gasped, or when her pupils would dilate. I let her set the pace, needing this time to be less about the destination and more about us coming together as a couple. Fusing the two of us together.

Her eyelids started to flutter and she fought them closing. Her thighs clenched around my hips and her whole body began to shake. "Austin..."

"I know, sweetheart. I've got you." I put both my hands on her hips to help her keep her rhythm. Then she tossed her head back and I felt her squeeze me from the inside. Her moan was like music, making me feel like the most powerful man in the world. I held myself back and made sure she rode out her orgasm before I spilled myself into her, her name on my lips, over and over.

We held each other until we grew cold and my legs went

numb. I pulled down the sheets and climbed in, pulling her against me and holding her tight.

"No take-backsies tomorrow, okay?"

She snorted. "What, are we five?"

I poked her side. "Pinkie swear, missy."

She laughed like I knew she would and we both fell asleep with permanent smiles.

19

Elle

I woke up to loud snoring in my ear and something stiff against my backside. I pushed back my hips, thinking he'd quit sawing logs. Instead, Austin laughed and flipped me onto my back with lightning speed, settling between my thighs.

"I'm just teasing. I'm twenty-two. I don't snore like an old man yet." Austin's dimples winked at me, wishing me a good morning. I strained my neck to place a kiss on each one.

"Why do you keep doing that? Is that a Spanish thing?"

I giggled, insanely happy to be starting my day with him. "No! It's a 'you have adorable dimples and I've started an affair with them' thing."

He frowned and they went away. "I don't know how I feel about you cheating on me so soon in our relationship." Then he smiled and they were back.

I cleared my throat. "Speaking of..." Nothing to do but just throw it out there and see what he said. "I would like to meet your sister." As much as I wanted to hide away where I wouldn't have to see him shutter his eyes and refuse to let me in, I tilted my head up and looked at him squarely. I'd run away before. I wasn't going to do that again.

He nodded once. "Done. We'll go today."

I blinked. "B-but that's it?"

He chuckled, the rumble in his chest sending flutters through my belly. "Yes, of course I want you to meet my sister. We're a couple now, right?" A look of horror flitted across his face. "*Right?*"

"Yes," I was quick to reassure him. "I just didn't think you'd let me in so quickly after everything I've done."

His eyes softened and he spoke softly. "Elle, I love you. That's what you do with people you love. You let them in." Then he tilted his hips and the fluttering soared to new levels. "In every way."

When we came up for air much later, he called his sister, waking her up and explaining where he was. He'd texted her last night when we walked back to the hotel, but she hadn't seen his text as she was still sleeping. He teased her about being a sleepy-head and I could hear the affection in his voice. I went to take a shower, suddenly nervous to meet this girl he loved so much.

Would she like me? Would I be super awkward and weird around her, or push her away without meaning to? I started thinking about what outfit I should wear, like putting on armor to engage the enemy. But when I caught sight of my naked self in the mirror, makeup-less and hair a tangled mess, I realized I didn't want to live that way any longer. I had a chance to love and be loved by a man like Austin. I didn't need armor to meet his sister. I simply needed to be me.

The open-air patio was one of the things I loved most about

Southern California restaurants. The weather was almost always ideal for eating outside, even if space heaters or sun shades had to be installed to keep it open year-round. This one had made use of multiple water features, which drowned out the sound of the traffic on the nearby freeway.

Austin insisted this was his and his sister's new favorite spot to grab some food. We'd made arrangements to meet here for lunch, allowing us all time to get ready. Abi didn't have a car yet, so Austin chose the restaurant because it was walking distance from their shared apartment.

It was hard to believe someone as young as Austin had custody of a teen. Most twenty-two-year-olds were still partying late at night and half-heartedly seeking jobs to pay the bills. Austin had his own place, a steady high-paying job, and a sixteen-year-old to look after. Kind of embarrassing to admit I'd attempted having a pet once, only to have the damn goldfish go belly up a week after being in my care. It was easy to forget the ten-year age difference between us when Austin was so responsible.

We sat across from each other at a table for four. I sipped my glass of ice water, leg bouncing up and down as we waited for Abi.

Austin grabbed my hand and held it on the table, his thumb sweeping across my skin. "Hey, she's gonna love you. Don't worry."

I gave him a shaky smile and then his gaze went over my head, his dimples reappearing in full force. Showtime.

Austin stood and hugged the girl who came up to our table in a cloud of PINK perfume and ripped jeans that should be illegal on a minor.

"Abi, I'd like you to meet my girlfriend, Elle." Austin pulled back, his arm around his sister while he gestured over to me. I stood and extended my hand, the nerves of meeting her overpowering the pleasure of hearing him call me his girlfriend for the first time.

The blonde bombshell didn't even glance at my hand, just rushed forward and pulled me into a hug. I was shocked for a split second before my brain kicked into gear. Of course she would hug me. Her brother was the king of huggers. I wrapped my arms around her and gave her a big squeeze in return, the butterflies leaving immediately.

We all had smiles as we sat down, Abi between us.

"So. Girlfriend, huh?" She winked at Austin, but turned back to me, her blue eyes sparkling so very much like Austin's.

I nodded, figuring honesty was the best avenue. "Yes, he accepted my apology and we're together now."

She pointed back and forth between Austin and me. "So, how exactly is this gonna work? You're on the East Coast, right?" Then she spun to Austin, her jaw dropped open. "We're not moving again, are we? School starts next week!"

He sat forward and grabbed her hand. "No, we're not moving." Then he looked at me. "We're not really sure how this is going to work, but we'll figure it out together. Date long distance. Take things slow."

I agreed with him. "My new restaurant still needs me, so I'll be there quite a bit, but we'll fly back and forth as opportunity allows. But I want you to know, Abi, I have no intention of uprooting you. I know you're just getting settled here and that will always be a priority."

Abi stared at me, her blue eyes wide. She seemed to be assessing me, maybe determining if what I said was the truth. Then her eyes filled with tears and she blinked rapidly, nodding. "Okay," she whispered.

The server came to take our order and we settled into easy chatter for the rest of lunch. If there had been any sort of test, I'd passed with flying colors. And in all honesty, Abi was a darling. She was spirited and lively, her hands and face expressive while she listened and especially while she talked. She was an interesting combination of both wildly confident and completely naive. I wanted to shelter her and be a big sister to her, if she'd let me.

"Excuse me." A young couple approached our table, the woman clutching her hands under her chin. "Are you guys the chefs on that new show, by any chance?"

Austin looked at me bewildered and I stared right back. Could she be—was she talking about Taste Test? My brain took a while to catch on, but then I remembered the commercials and the debut airing tonight.

"Yes, hello. I'm Elle Fierro." I stood and shook her hand. She was positively giddy to meet me. "And this is Austin Cox." I gestured to Austin and he stood to shake her hand too. His dimples were out, so the woman couldn't help but gush over him, her poor husband standing by awkwardly.

"Here! Let me get a picture of you all." Abi hopped up and waved to the woman for her cell phone. I moved next to Austin and he put his arm around both me and the woman and smiled. This whole situation was so incredibly bizarre. Were we considered some level of celebrity now?

The woman squealed after Abi took the picture, positively beaming to have us on camera.

We thanked her for watching and she walked off, leaving us in a bubble of awkward silence. The three of us sat back down and looked at each other, our eyes a little glazed over.

"You think that's going to happen more often?" Austin asked me.

I shook my head. "I have no idea, but I guess so. I kind of forgot the premiere is tonight." I looked over at Abi. "Should we have a watch party at your place?"

She nearly bounced out of her chair, her face split with a grin. "Yes! This is great! Let's get a bunch of food and we'll watch it together! What do you say, Austin? Pajama party?"

I tossed my head back and laughed. What could he possibly say to that? He was going to have a tough two years on his hands. Saying no—ever—to that face and that enthusiasm might be impossible.

Austin was looking at me from across the table while I laughed, his gaze intense. His look made me shiver even though I was plenty warm on the inside. I sobered quickly and smiled back shyly.

"I love you," he said, voice low and gravelly, meant just for me.

"I love you too."

"Oh my God, you two are ridiculously cute!" Abi squealed, breaking our moment. "And kind of gross, I have to admit. Can we go now?"

"You bet, Abilene. Gotta go get our pajamas ready for the big watch party, huh?" Austin stood, putting his arm around his sister and rubbing the top of her head. I winced, seeing her cute bun slipping to the side of her head, knowing no woman appreciated a noogie in the middle of a restaurant.

"Oof!" Austin let go of her and grabbed his ribs where Abi had elbowed him.

The glare on her face while she fixed her bun made my heart literally sigh in my chest seeing how much they loved each other. Which just made me love Austin even more. I wanted to be part of their circle. I wanted to tease them and for them to feel comfortable teasing me. They were a family of two and I'd give anything to make it a family of three.

We exited the restaurant and started walking down the sidewalk to their apartment, Austin and I hand in hand. A man in sweats jumped out from a car and heaved a huge black camera in front of his face and started clicking. We skidded to a stop and then Austin dropped my hand and put it on my low back, urging me to walk faster.

"Wha—" I felt like a fish, my mouth flopping open but no words coming out.

"Come on, Elle. Just part of the deal." I swiveled my head in a daze, seeing Austin's jaw clenched tight and his other hand pushing his sister to keep walking.

"Wait! We just want to know about your show! Airs tonight, right?" the camera guy yelled after us and my brain finally caught up to what was happening.

I planted my feet, which wasn't easy in heels—yes, of course I wore heels to lunch—and turned around to face the paparazzi.

"Wait, Austin. We shouldn't run away. Let's give them a nice picture."

Austin looked at me with questions in his eyes, but I gave him a confident smile. If they wanted a picture, we should give them a good one. The way I saw it, this was the perfect time to come out about our relationship.

"Hi! Yes, the show starts tonight. Can you send me a copy of our picture?"

"Oh, you bet. Thank you for stopping. Here's my card." The guy dug in his pocket and handed me his business card.

I looked down at the white square and then pulled Austin to my side, wrapping my arms around his waist and snuggling into his side. "Well, Harry, you're my first paparazzi. Make sure you get my good side, no?"

He chuckled and lifted the camera again. "You don't have a bad side, Ms. Fierro. Are you Austin Cox?" *Click, click.*

Austin's hand curled around my shoulder. "Yes, nice to meet you, Harry."

"So, are you two a couple?" Harry's gaze flicked between the two of us.

"Yes, aren't they adorable?" Abi came up next to Austin and beamed at Harry. "I'm Abi, Austin's sister. I can't wait to see their show tonight. Are you going to watch it?"

Harry looked stunned by Abi. She seemed to have that effect on people. Hard to believe she was in foster care for almost two months and yet seemed to have no ill side effects from the experience. "Um, well, sure. Now that I've met you guys, I'll be sure to check it out."

"Awesome! Here, let's get a shot of all three of us, huh?" She tucked her arm through Austin's and we all smiled for Harry.

A few more pleasantries, and we were again on our way to Austin and Abi's apartment.

"Did that just happen?" I asked no one in particular.

Austin kissed the side of my head while we walked. "Are you sure you're okay? Everyone's going to know we're together now."

I squeezed him tighter. "I've never been so sure of anything before. I love you and I don't care who knows."

His eyes flared with a light I'd come to recognize. He nuzzled in closer and whispered in my ear. "Any chance we can get my sister out of the house so I can strip you naked? Pretty please?"

I giggled, my heart light, the world in full color, and my passion fully restored. I'd gotten it wrong, though. It wasn't Austin who changed it all for me, it was love.

EPILOGUE

ustin

Elle's flight was landing any minute. I'd taken the night off work in preparation for her arrival. Abi was staying the night at a friend's house and I had plans to make tonight special for Elle and me.

True to her word, Elle had put in effort all year to make sure we spent as much time together as possible, even with our restaurant responsibilities and my vow to make Abi a priority. Elle had embraced our relationship like a duck to water, empowering her executive chef to run her restaurant without her most of the time and integrating into our life here in California.

Most surprising was that when the public heard about us right before the premiere, they went nuts over the cute new "it" couple. Much to Elle's embarrassment, I "accidentally" dropped our name to the press and we were permanently dubbed "Team FieryCox" in all news articles.

The studio loved us even more, seeing how we brought in

more press to the Taste Test show. Tom was asked to bring the show back for a second and third season. Elle was invited to return as one of the celebrity judges. When she heard that Michael Fin was not also invited, she agreed—with a pay increase—and spent most of her time in Southern California, which suited me just fine. The camera loved her, and with her happier disposition, the television audience loved her too. My El Jefe was world famous.

Two months ago, we agreed that my apartment was too small for all three of us, what with Elle there almost all the time. So we went in together on a new condo not far from the beach in Santa Monica. Abi kept all her same friends since we stayed near her high school and she loved having them over to our new place, showing off the gourmet kitchen we'd renovated before we even moved in.

Speaking of Abi, she was "living her best life" as she put it. She'd made friends easily her junior year in a new school. Elle and Abi had become instant friends, Elle being like a big sister to her. In fact, Elle had started taking her to the studio in Burbank on occasion, which Abi loved. I'd had a talent agent call me to see if he could get Abi on his roster as he just knew he could get her onto a television show. I hadn't made a decision on that yet. Right now, Abi was on her best behavior trying to win my favor and that was behavior I could live with for a while, even if it kept her in limbo.

Life was so good, I almost had to pinch myself on a daily basis. My heart had returned to my chest the instant Elle came back into my life. And then I'd subsequently handed it over to her for safekeeping. I'd never regretted that decision. Which made my decision to move forward with my plan tonight an easy one.

I heard the door crack open and Elle dump her suitcase on the tile floor by the front door. "I'm home, *¡mi amor!*" Her voice carried all the way into the kitchen where I was putting our huge

Dutch bakeware into the preheated oven. I was trying out a new Cornish hen recipe, which wouldn't be done for two hours.

I wiped my hands and met her at the door to the kitchen, picking her up and spinning her around. She yelped and clutched my shoulders, her surprise turning to smiles.

"That's quite a welcome home. I was only gone two days," she teased.

"Hell yes, woman. I've got a whole date night planned for you and me. I intend to woo your dress off you tonight."

She lifted an eyebrow, making that face that always turned me on and made me want to lasso the moon for her. Right before throwing her on the nearest surface and having my way with her.

"Oh, really? That must be some grade-A wooing."

"Wait and see." I set her down and grabbed my keys. "But first, we have to take a quick trip." Snagging her favorite flip-flops from the bin by the door, I set them on the floor for her to change into. Where we were going, high heels wouldn't do.

I tugged her behind me and folded her into my car. Running around the hood, I slid behind the wheel and sped off to destinations unknown.

"You going to tell me where we're going?"

"Not a chance." I grabbed her hand and held it on my thigh, loving having the control. It drove her nuts not to know what was going on. Which made me do it more, of course, just to hear her curse in Spanish.

We pulled up to the curb and I cut the engine. I brought her hand up to my mouth and kissed the back. "Promise to keep an open mind?" My heart was tripping over itself, not from nerves, but from excitement.

She narrowed her eyes, but a smile tugged at her lips. I climbed out of the car and went around to open her door. When she stood up, I clasped her hand in mine and moved out of the way so she could see where we were.

Directly in front of us was a decrepit old red brick building. It had seen better days—and not recently—but it was located right on the water. You could hear the waves lapping onto the sand from here.

"What is this place, Austin?" Elle was staring up at the building, not moving nor making any kind of facial expression to clue me into her thoughts.

"This old wreck right here is my little slice of heaven. I found it not too long ago and asked around. It's abandoned, owned by a trust somewhere on the East Coast. I have paperwork at the house just waiting for our signatures. If you want it, it's ours." I couldn't look away from her. Even in the condition it was in, Elle looked at home here.

She took a deep breath and held it. When she finally blew it out, she asked the right question. "Ours to do what with?"

"You and me, sweetheart. It's time we opened up our own restaurant together, don'tcha think?" I squeezed her hand and she whipped her head to look at me, eyes wide. "Do you trust me?"

"With everything," was her immediate answer.

My heart soared. "Then let's do this. Together."

She finally moved, her grin dazzling in intensity. She jumped into my arms and wrapped her legs around my waist. If I wasn't so taken by the moment and her acceptance, I would have teased her about her ability to jump so high for such a short, little thing.

As it was, her kisses peppered my face and I staggered back to bump into the brick wall. We proceeded to make out like teenagers up against the sturdy wall of our shared dream.

When a whistle from a passerby broke my consciousness, I set her down and pushed her away before I was arrested for public indecency. "Temptress..."

She licked her lips and smirked at me. So I did the only thing a hot-blooded male could do with that kind of temptation. I picked her up and tossed her over my shoulder. She whacked at my backside feebly and yelled unrepeatable things at me to put her down. Instead, I twirled us around right there on the sidewalk until I was in danger of dropping the most precious thing in the world. Then I put her in the car and raced us home.

She mistakenly believed that was the end of my wooing.

She was so very wrong.

I lit the candle on the dining table and served her my Cornish hen recipe to which she moaned and begged me to include that on the menu at our new restaurant. When I had her stomach full and satisfied I broke out the big guns.

"Go get into something more comfortable and meet me in the living room, would ya?" She knew I was up to something, but for once she kept her mouth closed and obeyed. Bossing around The Boss was always a tricky thing.

When she came back out in sexy lingerie I hadn't seen before, I nearly abandoned my plan like I'd abandoned the dirty dishes after dinner. But I had my eyes on the end game: making her mine forever.

"Sit down, love. I have to serve you dessert." I motioned toward the couch and made to go back into the kitchen.

"Wait, is this going to be like the pancakes where I need an industrial tarp and a hair net to sustain the onslaught of liquids?"

I barked out a laugh, looking over my shoulder. "That sounds so dirty, but no. Just you and the couch are needed."

When I came back out with my oversized plate, she was seated on the edge of the couch, her gorgeous body wrapped in lace like a present under the Christmas tree, ready for me to rip off and get my hands on what lay underneath.

"Focus on the end game, focus on the end game..." I muttered under my breath.

"What was that?"

I smiled, knowing I was on the verge of everything, and placed the platter on the coffee table in front of her. Her gaze dropped and she burst into laughter at my presentation. In a large heart shape were over two dozen small powder-covered donuts. I'd been stocking her favorite donut snacks in my cupboard since day one. Tonight, they spelled out my love for her.

She went to grab one and I stopped her. "Nuh-uh. Not that one." I pointed to the one at the bottom tip of the heart. "This one."

That eyebrow creeped up again, but she picked up the one I pointed to, stopping its descent to her mouth, frozen in her tracks.

Because on the platter, beneath her donut, was a ring.

A big gold ring with a huge square diamond winking at us.

I dropped to my knee and picked up the ring to offer it up to her. I bit back a smile seeing her frozen with her mouth open and a donut hanging out mid-air.

"Elle Fierro. You've lit my heart on fire since the moment I saw you in your underwear in that dressing room, telling me what an asshole I was. I can't imagine doing life without you. So I ask you to trust me, to promise to stick by my side, to live this life together. *Mi corazón es en fuego para ti.* Will you marry me?"

She finally unfroze and set the donut back on the table, before looking me in the eye. "Rule number nine: when you ask me to marry you, the answer will always be yes." She paused, her eyes misting over and her face softening. "Yes, Austin, I will marry you." Then she flung her arms around my neck and we held each other, neither one of us wanting to let go long enough to put the ring on her finger.

"Wait, does this mean you're expecting me to repeatedly ask you to marry me? 'Cause I'm not sure I can work up the nerve to do that again," Austin whispered in my ear.

"I won't make you do it again if you promise to never butcher that sentence again," she whispered back.

I pulled back to frown at her. "What? You didn't like that? I said my heart is on fire for you."

She nodded gravely. "Yes, I know that's what you tried to say, but maybe stick to English, no?"

I pursed my lips. "So, *¿no vamos a joder?*"

She let a giggle slip out. "*No, mi amor. Vamos a hacer el amor.*"

So we did.

Forever.

185

Don't forget to preorder Mom-Com, the second book in the Reality of Love series, while it's only $2.99! Keep reading for the first chapter sample...

NOTE FROM THE AUTHOR

Thank you so much for reading The Missing Ingredient! If you loved it, please support the series by leaving a review on <u>Amazon</u> or <u>Goodreads</u> so other readers can find it and enjoy it too. Reviews help other readers determine if a book is to their liking and they help indie authors sell more books so we can keep writing. If you hated it, please disregard this entire paragraph. :)

If you'd like to know more about me or the other novels that I'm writing, please come ~~stalk~~ find me on <u>Facebook,</u> or my private <u>Reader Group</u>, or you can find me in-person, on the beach in Southern California, frolicking like a Baywatch babe.

I'm everywhere....
Amazon - https://www.amazon.com/author/marikaray

Goodreads -
https://www.goodreads.com/author/show/16856659.Marika_Ray

Bookbub - https://www.bookbub.com/authors/marika-ray

Instagram - https://www.instagram.com/authormarikaray

Twitter - https://www.twitter.com/authormarikaray

Pinterest - https://www.pinterest.com/marikarayauthor/

Book + Main - https://bookandmainbites.com/MarikaRay

READING ORDER

<u>Steamy RomComs:</u>
Happy New You
Mom-Com - Reality of Love #2-May 2019
Closing Costs - Reality of Love #3-Sept 2019

<u>Sweet Romances:</u>
The Marriage Sham
The Widower's Girlfriend-Faking It #1-April 2019
Home Run Fiance - Faking #2-June 2019

<u>Beach Squad Series/Steamy Beach Romance:</u>
1) Sweet Dreams
2) Beach B!tch
3) Barefoot Chaos
* Novella - Handcuffed Hussy
4) Beach Bum Billion-Heiress
5) Brighter Than the Boss
* Novella - Christmas Eve Do-Over

SCENE FROM MOM-COM

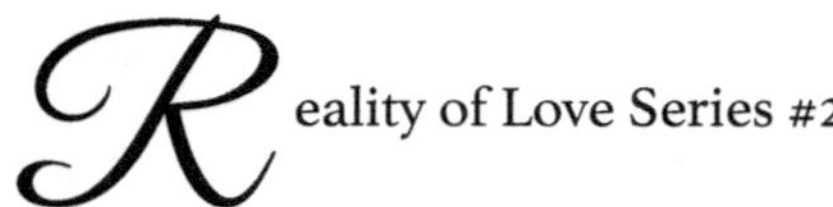

eality of Love Series #2

Lily-Marie

I clicked the door shut behind me, wishing I could slam it instead and get out some of the frustration bubbling inside me. With my two kids asleep in their beds—dear God, please say they were asleep—a soft click would have to do. That's why moms drank wine. It was silent, tasty, and calmed the daily frustrations that chafed almost as badly as the Spanx trying to hold in my poochy belly those same kids were responsible for.

We couldn't have tantrums so we drank. Sue me.

"Gabby?" I whisper-yelled into my house.

My lifelong best friend was babysitting for me tonight so I could "enjoy" a night out with a guy I'd connected with on Kinder, the latest dating app that promised "solid relationships with just one click!" More like false promises and nightmares. Bejeezus, why were people so weird? Was it too much to ask to be swept off one's feet by a dashing prince? Although, I guess that wasn't Kinder's fault. Maybe I should blame the company I happened to work for. I mean, they kind of sold me—even as a little girl—on the idea of a prince saving me with one perfect kiss.

"Hey, how did it go?" Gabby came around the corner, rubbing her eyes. She checked the watch on her wrist, frowning.

I hung my jacket up on the hook by the door and moved further into the house.

"Yeah, it's early, I know. Sorry to interrupt your nap. It was a lukewarm date right up until he whipped out his phone over the appetizers and showed me—and I'm not kidding you—at least thirty dick pics. Apparently, there's an art form for taking just the right one, did you know?" Her job dropped open and I continued. That joy needed to be spread. "Because, as I learned, lighting, angle, level of excitement, the temperature in the room. Those are all things that can positively or negatively affect the end result. Which. He. Showed. Me."

My eyes glazed over and I full body shivered just recalling the things I'd seen. Gabby snapped her mouth closed and hustled around me to the kitchen, pulling down a bottle of wine from the top cabinet that had seen better days. At some point I'd get around to refacing my cabinets. Tonight was not that day.

"I know what this calls for. Tonight's a merlot night." She pulled out two glasses and got to work on the cork.

I sank into a bar stool and pushed the kids' stack of graded homework out of the way. "God bless you." My shoes, the ones I only pulled out for dates because they killed my feet, were kicked off in a frenzy. And then, only because we were such good friends and I had enough dirt on her to last a lifetime, I reached up under my dress and peeled off the Spanx so I could breathe.

"Oh, that's nice..." I whispered, sitting back down and

accepting the glass she held out to me. The first sip went down the hatch and I could feel the layer of ick he'd left on me with his detailed pictures sliding off my skin, hopefully never to be seen again.

"That's truly the most disgusting thing I've heard recently. And I just babysat your eight-year-old son who thought it was fun to make slime and smear it all over his skin like he was a mutant lizard shedding his winter coat." Gabby sat on the stool next to me, her long black hair always so perfect, even though she'd just woken up after babysitting the hellion spawn of mine I loved so dearly.

I cringed. "Ah, conned you into making slime again, huh?"

She shrugged. "It made him happy and you know I can't say no to my god-children." She raised her glass and we clinked them together before taking another healthy swig. "So, fill me in. How have the other dates gone?"

Gabby was a hot shot columnist for the LA Times, writing a modern day advice column, similar to Ann Landers, but with a younger perspective. She was busy all the time, but still found time to encourage—nag—me about going on dates with men I met online.

I'd been single for two years, but was just now feeling like dating men was something I was ready for. I'd only been with my ex, having dated him all through high school and most of college before we had kids together. We never officially got married, and that was something that had always bothered me. Call me old fashioned, but I really wanted to wear a white dress and show off my sparkling diamond wedding ring. Which, if these recent dates were any indication, wouldn't be happening any time soon. My cabinets would getting that remodel before I was a Mrs.

"Oh God, Gabby. It's so bad out there. Seriously. Count yourself lucky you have a man already." I rubbed my forehead, smearing the makeup I'd so carefully applied just a few hours before. She didn't say anything so I kept spewing, the words leaking out uncensored. This was what I needed. Time with my bestie. Total therapy. "So, I went on that mid-day coffee date last week and I should have known better. He never showed. And here's the kicker: his *mom* showed up to tell me he couldn't make it."

Gabby drew her head back sharply. "No!"

I slapped a hand down on the counter and immediately winced at the noise it made, hurrying on in a whisper. "Yes! She said that he'd wrecked her car that morning and she took away his cell phone as punishment. Then she proceeded to tell me how wonderful he normally is and that I should call him in two days when she gave him back his cell phone."

Gabby's giggle turned into a full-out belly laugh. She abandoned her wine glass on the counter and bent over, muffling her laugh with her knees.

"It's not funny!" I whisper-yelled at the top of her head. "Besides, you're going to want to hear what happened with my lunch date."

Her head whipped up and she swiped the tears from her wide eyes. "It gets worse?"

I take the time to top off my glass before answering. She laughed at me. She can wait a minute or two before I tell her more. "As I was saying, I had a lunch date last week too. I showed up, he showed up. He was just as attractive as his picture so things were looking good, right? Next thing I know, he's telling me all about his last fight with his ex-girlfriend. And I mean details! Like his favorite red sundress she was wearing, and the way she called him an asshole under her breath which she knows he hates. By the time my salad showed up, I was ready to shovel it down and get the hell out of there."

"Wow, Lil, that's crazy. I wish I could say that's abnormal, but there are some crazy ass people out there." Gabby looks at me sympathetically. She gets a lot of crazies writing in and asking her for advice on bizarre life situations, so I knew she understood.

"But that's not even the end of it." I placed my glass on the counter. I needed two hands for this. "By the time I ate my salad, he'd let the cat out of the bag that he and his girlfriend were *still together*. They hadn't actually broken up. I was out on a lunch date helping a guy cheat on his girlfriend."

"Oh, honey..." Gabby looked a little green. That was an area we'd always agreed on: cheating was never okay. Not ever.

"But wait!" I stopped talking and burst out laughing. "Oh, my God! I sound like an infomercial. 'But wait, there's more!'" Gabby laughed with me and then I finished it. "So, naturally, I hop up like my chair's on fire and head out the door. He follows me all the way to my car and tries to hug me. I push him off me, but his hand is stuck in my purse. The fucker was trying to pick pocket me on our cheating date!"

Gabby jumped off the stool and looked ready to fight the dude right there on the spot. "What did you do?"

"I slapped his hand away from my purse, kicked him in the nuts, and drove off."

We bumped fists and settled back down on our stools to sip our wine and calm down.

"I feel highly compelled to write about this, you know that, right?" Gabby looked at me, pleading with her dark eyes.

I shook my head. "I'm sorry, but my pathetic dating life can't be in your column. My fragile ego can't handle it."

"Even if it's anonymous?"

"Even if it's anonymous. *I'd* know, Gabby." I sighed. "After Shawn, I just don't know if I can handle more of a spotlight on my single hood, you know?"

Her hand rubbed my back. "I know. I promise I won't write anything. The last thing I want to do is discourage you from getting back out there. Shawn wasn't your forever, but your forever is out there somewhere waiting for you. I just know it." She pulled me into a side hug. "I'm proud of you, Lil."

"Thanks, Gabriella. I'm proud of me for trying too. When

Shawn left, I was shocked. I thought we'd be together forever. I never envisioned being a single mom and trying to date thirty-somethings who were passed over or left behind. They all have this desperation that clings to them like a bad odor." Oh jeez, I needed to put down the wine before I got any more poetic.

"What I'm trying to say is I just don't think this app thing is going to work. The kind of guy I'm looking for doesn't live with his mama and he surely doesn't need to pick pocket me to pay his rent. I need a man who sweeps me off my feet and only has eyes for me. He'll take one look at me and my children and want to put a big rock on my finger. And if he's really awesome, he'll snuggle with me and watch Disney princess movies. Is that too much to ask?"

Gabby went surprisingly serious on me, even though I handed her the perfect opportunity to tease me about my princess obsession. "No, that's not too much to ask. In fact, I think we should have always been demanding that. Maybe our problem has always been not asking for enough." Before I could examine that nugget of wisdom or ask how things were going with Hew, her boyfriend, she hopped off the stool and started gathering her things. "Gotta go, girlie. Got words to write and hours to toss and turn before my alarm goes off."

I made a mental note to sit her down soon and see if things were rocky with her and Hewitt. They'd been together for a year, maybe not blissfully happy, but steady none-the-less. She hadn't said anything outright, but my best friend radar was beeping. Something wasn't right with her and I intended to get to the bottom of it.

I walked her out and made sure she got on the road safe. Then I locked up, turned out lights, and headed up to kiss my babies goodnight. They wouldn't remember, but I couldn't help myself. They gave me gray hairs, but I loved them fiercely. Sleep wouldn't come if I didn't check on them and give them the kisses they wouldn't normally stand still long enough for when they were awake.

Clark was flat on his back, arms and legs spread like he'd squeezed every last drop of life out of the day before flopping back on his mattress and conking out. I pulled the sheets from under his legs and covered him up, my movements not even stirring him. He was still so small at eight years old, even as he tried to act like the man of the house with his father gone. Sure, he saw his dad every other weekend, but in between those times, he was trying to act older. Why, I didn't know, but I hoped he stayed a kid for as long as he could.

I tip-toed into Milly's room, skipping over the wood board that creaked. She slept light and was hard to creep in on. There'd already been some near misses on Christmas Eve when I'd been trying to get her presents under the tree from Santa and she'd heard me.

My beautiful girl had big, blonde curls that reminded me of myself at that age. I'd learned to control them with product, but on a five-year-old, they were adorable and wild. I brushed the barest of kisses on her forehead and backed away slowly.

It was moments like these that made everything right in my world. I had my kids. I had my health. Everything would be fine.

In my own bedroom, I put on my cotton pajama pants and ratty, old tank top before snuggling under the covers and clicking on the TV with the remote. I hit play and smiled as the opening credits to Sleeping Beauty floated softly through the speakers. I was the proud owner of every Disney princess movie on DVD. Some women needed Ambien to sleep. I needed happy ever afters and Prince Charming.

The melodic notes of *I Wonder* flowed over me as Aurora sang to the forest animals. My eyes began to blink shut as I commiserated with her. She wondered where her someone was and so did I.

Fumbling with the remote, I finally shut it off and drifted to sleep, visions of princesses and handsome princes filling my head. Except in my dreams, one of the handsome men was for little, old me. He picked me up and swung me around at a fancy ball, my children on the sidelines smiling from ear to ear. A diamond ring sat on my finger as he pulled me in for a kiss...